1

SHADOW ON THE LAKE

SHADOW ON THE LAKE

Mary Mackie

Chivers Press • Thorndike Press
Bath, England   Thorndike, Maine USA

This Large Print edition is published by Chivers Press, England, and by Thorndike Press, USA.

Published in 1999 in the U.K. by arrangement with the author.

Published in 1999 in the U.S. by arrangement with Lawrence Pollinger, Ltd.

583389

U.K. Hardcover ISBN 0–7540–3597–2 (Chivers Large Print)
U.K. Softcover ISBN 0–7540–3598–0 (Camden Large Print)
U.S. Softcover ISBN 0–7862–1669–7 (General Series Edition)

MORAY COUNCIL

Department of Technical

& Leisure Services

The text of this Large Print edition is unabridged.
Other aspects of the book may vary from the original edition.

F

Set in 16 pt. New Times Roman.

Printed in Great Britain on acid-free paper.

British Library Cataloguing in Publication Data available

Library of Congress Cataloging-in-Publication Data

Mackie, Mary.
    Shadow on the lake / by Mary Mackie.
       p.   cm.
    ISBN 0–7862–1669–7 (lg. print : sc : alk. paper)
    1. Large type books.   I. Title.
    [PR6063.A2454S52   1999]
    823'.914—dc21   98–31300

CHAPTER ONE

The view from my hotel balcony was breathtaking. Palm trees swayed gently, fanning the deep blue bay, and the lights of Lisbon were strung out below me like diamond necklaces flung down at random. The air was warm, heady with subdued excitement—but I found myself wondering what I was doing there.

David Elliott was the cause of my presence in Lisbon. He had called, asking me to come, and I had taken the first plane, like the devoted little slave I was. For three years he had had this power over me, ever since he exploded into my life when I was lonely and bewildered, trying to make my way as an actress after being 'discovered' in a crowd scene.

David had seemed so wonderful. He was handsome, charming, assured, and I had been overwhelmed. When I realized that he practised his mesmerism on every female he met, it was already too late. I was ensnared, grateful for every moment he allowed me, and willing to suffer the indignity of having him drop me or pick me up as the mood took him. Other women came and went in his life—I seemed a permanent fixture. Only recently had I realized that my attraction for him existed

1

solely in the fact that I refused to sleep with him. David was not accustomed to being refused.

Yet still I came when he called. He missed me, he said. He wanted me to be in the pits during tomorrow's race. It was lovely in Lisbon. We could have a marvellous time.

The flight had been bumpy and David neglected to meet me. Instead, I was accosted by a reporter who recognized me. I was flattered, until I realized that the reporter was not interested in me for myself, but for my relationship with the glamorous racing driver. Fending off the questions, I made for the hotel where David had reserved a room for me next to his and found, not an eagerly-waiting David, but a message for me to meet him at the race track that afternoon.

When I arrived at the track, I found David with a dark-eyed senorita hanging on to his every word. He greeted me as casually as if I were his sister whom he had seen an hour before, and then he was off, in a cloud of noise and fumes, for a practice session, leaving me with the mechanics and Lucia, who would willingly have killed me if her glances at me were any indication.

I spent the afternoon in the pits thinking dark thoughts about David. The truth about him had penetrated at last. He was childish, selfish, bad-tempered. It was time I came to my senses.

2

But I decided to give him one final chance. That evening, having spent a great deal of time making myself attractive, I went down to the bar, where David was holding court amid a gathering of other drivers and a flurry of female admirers. His latest acquisition, Lucia, was draped on the arm of his chair wearing a scarlet dress of extreme décolletage.

I might have stuck it out but for the appearance of the reporter I had seen at the airport. He made a bee-line for me and stood talking, ostensibly fawning on me, but asking personal questions with a kind of veiled insolence at which my pride rose up in revolt. I walked out.

It was an hour before David noticed my absence and came looking for me, to inquire if I were ill. When I told him I was tired of being a hanger-on, he looked upset. He put his arms round me and kissed me sweetly and begged me to try and understand that it was necessary for him to socialize. People expected it of him. He must keep up appearances. And I, fool that I was, relented. David could be so tender when he tried, so plausible. I let him kiss and caress me out of my unreasonable mood.

Then he made the mistake of trying to unzip my dress. Instantly, I was on my guard and pushed him forcibly from me.

'You *are* in a mood,' he said disgustedly, turning to the door. 'And you can stew in it. Perhaps tomorrow you'll have settled down.'

So he left me. After a while, I went out on to the balcony and stood there looking at that lovely view while I examined my feelings and motives. I was still very fond of David. He was my rock. Who else was there to turn to? I rarely saw my mother since the terrible day I quarrelled with my step-father and left home. There was no one else. No one I could call friend. Except David. Perhaps if I gave him what he wanted . . .

I don't know how long I had been standing there, but it must have been almost midnight when I heard voices in the next room, David's room, whose balcony door was wide open. The room itself was in darkness, but the whispers told me it was occupied. And then I heard Lucia's husky laughter and David's voice, murmuring love words.

Of course I knew how he carried on with his women, but he had never been so blatant before. He must have known I would still be in my room. This was his way of paying me out.

I couldn't take any more. Hurrying down to the reception, I booked a seat on the early morning flight to England. David was still in bed when I left the hotel.

Back in London, I phoned my agent. No, there were no offers, unless I was prepared to do nude love scenes. I wasn't. Obviously I was too old-fashioned to exist in this permissive age. I settled down with a newspaper, dismally scanning the 'Situations Vacant'.

*   *   *

On the side table in the flat, beside the telephone, was a large framed photograph of David. I had put it there deliberately, so that when he phoned I could talk to his picture. In it, he was smiling his own attractive seductive smile and his wavy dark hair was combed into unnatural neatness. I was able now to look at the photograph with detachment and it was some time before I registered the absence of the sick longing which always used to assail me when he was away. Far from missing him, I was relieved to be rid of the seething emotions he aroused when he was near. Perhaps I was really over him this time.

As I sat exploring this strange new feeling, the telephone rang. It was David.

'What got into you?' he demanded. 'I was counting on you being in the pits to cheer me on. The race starts in an hour.'

'I know,' I said. 'Good luck.'

'Is that all you've got to say? I suppose you know that if I crash it will be your fault. Why did you walk out on me?'

'I had to. I finally realized it was no use. And don't try to pretend you're upset. If you cared one hoot for me I wouldn't have left. But you don't. So I did. You won't crash, David. In an hour's time you'll have forgotten my existence.'

5

His tone changed. He dropped the outrage and tried cajoling. 'That isn't true, darling. I miss you. I'm sorry if I upset you. Please say you forgive me. Look, I'll be back in a couple of days and we'll do the town together, shall we?'

'Call me when you get here,' I said calmly, 'but I don't guarantee to be available. 'Bye, David.'

'Carole!' That was all I heard as I replaced the receiver.

I felt strangely calm about it all. It was funny how love could just die, without warning. One day you cared, the next you didn't. Sad, really, except that I didn't believe love behaved that way. Infatuation, yes, fascination, physical attraction, but not love. Ergo, I had not loved David. Funny how one can delude oneself.

I took myself shopping, to celebrate the end of my 'David phase' and returned to the flat feeling free and light-headed. I sang along with Radio One and even tried out a few original dance undulations as I waited for my eggs to boil. It was ages since I had been so carefree.

The hourly News Bulletin came on, but I wasn't really listening, until the announcement of a piece of late news from Lisbon made me prick up my ears.

'British racing driver David Elliott was injured today when his car spun from the track and burst into flames. We hope to have further details in our next bulletin at 6.30.'

6

With a blast of music, the disc jockey started burbling again, unconcernedly. I snapped off the radio and stood staring at the wall, unable to believe my ears. From somewhere far off I seemed to hear David's voice, saying, 'If I crash, it will be your fault.' And he had crashed. David?

'David?' I said aloud, and the sound of my horrified voice brought me to my senses. I plunged for the phone, frantically dialling Overseas Enquiries.

After several frustrating minutes, I found myself talking to Joe Mears, David's head mechanic.

'Is he badly hurt?' I demanded hysterically.

'Bad enough,' came Joe's flat North-country voice, distorted by distance. 'Cuts and bruises and his hands were burned.'

'Do you think I ought to come?' I asked.

'No. He said if you rang I was to say he'll be home in a few days. You shouldn't have run out on him, Carole, not just before the race. He was real cut-up.'

My throat was choked with guilt and it was a few moments before I was able to say, 'Give him my love, Joe. Tell him I'll be waiting.'

'Aye,' said Joe. 'I'll do that.'

I was too wrought-up to think clearly. Whatever I felt for David, I didn't want him hurt, not like that, after a quarrel. I was ashamed of myself, sure that it was my fault. I made a vow that I would make it up to David

7

in whatever way I could.

Two days soul-searching went by. By the morning of the third day I was beginning to think more rationally and remember all the things about David that annoyed me. I was no longer convinced that I was responsible for the crash. If David cared enough to be upset when I left him, then he cared enough not to hurt me by running round with other women. But he didn't. I had had every right to walk out. He was self-centred, arrogant, disloyal . . .

And then the doorbell rang and David was standing there, looking pale and ill, a plaster across one temple and both hands enveloped in bandages. I took one look at the pitiful, anxious expression in his eyes and forgot all logic. My arms flew round his neck. I found myself apologizing incoherently, crying and laughing, kissing and being kissed, and suddenly nothing mattered but that he was here, the lovable David who could make me forget his alter ego.

'Am I forgiven?' he asked eventually, his arms still tightly around me.

'Of course,' I choked, rubbing my wet face on his jacket.

'Then will you please marry me?' David said.

I became still. Was I hearing things? Was this really David—proposing marriage?

'Carole?' he said anxiously. 'Did you hear what I said?'

'Yes.' I looked up into his serious, pleading face. 'But I . . .'

'Please,' David said softly, and put his mouth back on mine, kissing me hard and holding me so tightly I couldn't breathe. As always, I was lost in him, unable to think at all. When I could speak again, I breathed my acquiescence.

He released me slowly and asked me to reach inside his jacket pocket, where my fingers closed around a domed ring box.

'Well, open it,' he urged when I stood staring dumbly at the object in my hands.

Still feeling dazed, I lifted the lid of the box, revealing a ring with a solitaire diamond as big as a pea set in a gold claw.

'You were so sure, weren't you?' I said, my voice tinged with bitterness.

'No,' David said quickly. 'I had to make sure. Put it on, Carole. See if it fits.'

It did fit, and it was the loveliest thing I had ever owned. I was engaged, at last, to David Elliott.

*   *   *

We sat down to discuss the future. David favoured an autumn wedding. October, perhaps? No point in rushing into it. Besides— with a wry glance at his heavily bandaged hands—he wanted to be properly fit. We decided to shelve the matter of setting a date.

9

There were, however, more immediate plans to make. David would be out of racing for a while, and I wasn't working. Why didn't we spend the summer with his family in Cumberland?

I was surprised by this suggestion. David was David, an entity on his own, and his family were unimportant to me because they seemed unimportant to him. In the three years I had known him, he had rarely mentioned them.

'Your family?' I queried. 'Would they have us?'

'Why not?' David said blithely. 'They'll want to meet the girl I'm going to marry, and the house is plenty big enough. It's on Trentismere Lake, fairly secluded. My father runs a small boat-yard. Motor-boats, power-boats and things that they sell all over the North. The Elliotts are well known up there. It's a good business. Where did you think I got the money to start racing?'

'I never thought about it,' I said truthfully.

David smiled tenderly at me. 'It's time you started thinking. You must know all about my family now that we're getting married. And I want them to know you. You'll be able to witness the return of the prodigal.'

'Are you?' I said. 'The prodigal?'

David laughed and hugged me, clumsily because of his hands. 'Of course, darling. What else? Let's go tomorrow. Pack your things and bring them round to my flat. Come tonight, if you like.' His brown eyes were gleaming with amusement, but beneath it there lurked a predatory light I knew well and hated.

'No, David,' I said firmly.

His mouth twisted. 'Victorian to the end, aren't you, darling? All right, tomorrow it is. You won't mind driving, will you?'

When he was gone, I phoned my mother, who lived in Sussex with my step-father, with whom I shared a mutual hatred.

'I'm going to stay in Cumberland,' I told mother, 'with David's family.'

'That's nice,' mother said. 'How is David?'

She didn't really care how he was, so I said, 'Fine. We just got engaged.'

After a small silence, mother said vaguely, 'I thought you already were engaged. But, well, that's nice.'

'Thank you,' I said heavily, knowing the sarcasm would be lost on her, and adding, 'Give my love to Henry.'

She was silent again, but eventually said tautly, 'I wish you wouldn't be like that, Carole,' and put the phone down.

*   *   *

By mid-afternoon, we reached the end of the M6 and were into the Lake District, on narrow, crowded roads which reduced even David's Maserati Mistrale to a crawl. We were both tired and it didn't help when David started criticizing my driving and calling me 'woman!', a term he knew I disliked.

It was eight o'clock when we topped a final rise and saw Lake Trentismere lying in the valley below, its water half in sunshine, half in shadow. The hills around it raised craggy shoulders out of a cloak of lush trees, making the place look wild and lonely and beautiful.

The road plunged down between the trees, so that the lake was a tantalizing glimmer through the leaves, and it wasn't long before David was instructing me to turn off between gateless posts on to a stony drive that wound down through the trees towards a big old house that stood by the lakeside. Late sunlight gilded its tall chimneys and made a blinding light of a broad window set in the sloping roof. That was all I saw before I was swinging the wheel to follow the twisting track.

We pulled up in deep shadow, beneath trees that lent a gloomy air to the house, and I glanced at David, finding him smiling to himself as he surveyed his home, smiling with a sort of grim humour that made me feel apprehensive.

'Is this it?' I asked.

'It is.' He opened the door with his forearm and climbed out stiffly. I, too, was cramped, and glad of the chance to stretch my legs and look around.

A breeze shushed softly through the trees and I heard a skylark singing in the evening

12

sky, but the house remained silent, its windows blank and unwelcoming. I shivered as the dampness flowing from beneath the trees made me suddenly chilly.

'Do you think they're out?' I asked, but no sooner had the words been said than the door of the house opened and a girl came out, to stand staring at David.

She was tall and pretty, about my age, with flowing dark hair caught back in a pink band that matched her simple dress. She looked fresh and young, and startled.

'David?' she said quietly, her tone a question, then, 'David! Oh . . .' and she ran to him, into his arms that opened to receive and hold her. I heard David laugh softly and he half-turned, to wink at me over the girl's head.

As she drew away, a torrent of half-asked questions tumbled from her lips, until David laughed again and swung her round to face me.

'Say hello to Carole . . . Darling, this is my baby sister Sarah.'

Shyly, Sarah held out her hand. 'I've seen your picture in the paper.'

'I'm glad to know you,' I said. 'I do hope we aren't putting you out. David did say he had warned you we were coming.'

'I didn't actually say that,' David objected. 'Anyway, I wanted it to be a surprise. Sarah, Carole's finally agreed to marry me.'

'Oh,' said Sarah, with a vehement sincerity

13

that puzzled me, 'I am glad. That's wonderful news. Ben . . .' She stopped, looking uncomfortable.

'What about Ben?' David inquired, a hard note creeping into his voice.

Sarah shook her head. 'Nothing. Nothing at all. Let's not stand here talking. Come in and see Dad. He'll be so pleased you're home.'

She led the way into the house, which was furnished with more comfort than style. It was a place to be at ease in—a home where people lived happily together. Or so I thought.

The repeating rhythm of Ravel's 'Bolero' came softly from the sitting-room, whose broad window overlooked the lake. Chintz curtains and covers made the room bright and friendly, an atmosphere that was counteracted by the wariness in the eyes of the old man who swung his wheelchair round to face us.

'So you're back,' he said, exchanging a cool stare with David.

'What kind of a welcome is that?' David asked pleasantly. 'I've brought my fiancée to meet you. Carole, this is my father.'

I took a step forward, holding out my hand, which was taken in the old man's caloused one while his black eyes stared speculatively at me from beneath thick grey brows.

'How do you do,' I said formally, feeling unaccountably small and silly.

'Are you staying?' was the reply.

'Well, we . . .' I faltered.

14

'Of course they are,' Sarah said swiftly, coming to my side. 'Don't let Dad frighten you, Carole. He's always like that. But underneath it he's as soft as putty. Sit down and make yourself at home while I put some coffee on.'

My hand was released and I thought I saw a glimmer of a smile touch the old man's eyes before he turned his grey head to look at David.

'We heard there was an accident,' he said, indicating David's bandages. 'How bad is it?'

'Burns,' David said. 'No permanent damage.'

'And the car?'

David shrugged, sinking into a chair. 'It's a write-off.'

Following his example, I settled down in a corner of the settee, watching David's father in an effort to understand more of him. He had obviously been a big man once, but now spare flesh hung on his large-boned frame and I wondered if illness had confined him to the wheel-chair. His face might have been carved out of wood, the brow prominent over an aquiline nose and thin, bony cheeks, the mouth tight-lipped.

David was recounting his accident in detail when a movement in the doorway behind him drew my eyes from his handsome face. A man stood in the doorway—a big, dark man with curling black hair and a muscular frame clothed in oily overalls. His hawk-like face was

15

a younger and only slightly softer version of the old man's, and his eyes, as they stared at the back of David's head, seemed filled with malevolence, I saw him clench his big hands, saw the muscles of his jaw tighten.

The conversation ceased abruptly. David glanced at me, then swung round to face the newcomer, coming to his feet.

He said evenly, 'Hello, Ben.'

CHAPTER TWO

Ben inclined his head in greeting, releasing the tension which may have been only in my imagination.

'I had a feeling you'd come,' he said. 'Home to lick your wounds, are you?'

'Where else would I go?' David asked. 'I'd like you to meet my fiancée Carole Davies. Darling, this is my little brother Ben. He always was a surly devil.'

I nodded at Ben, smiling and hoping my uncertainty didn't show. 'Hello.'

'My pleasure, Miss Davies,' he said coolly. 'We've heard of you, of course. It's lucky the newspapers follow Dave around. Otherwise we'd think he was dead. Please excuse my overalls. If I had known the great man was returning I would have dressed accordingly.'

'In sackcloth and ashes,' David said dryly,

16

which made Ben glance at him with an unreadable expression in his dark eyes.

Sarah appeared behind him with a laden tray, saying, 'Oh, there you are, at last. Ben, do go and get out of those filthy overalls. David and Carole have just arrived and I shan't let you join us until you've washed and changed.'

'You're worse than a nagging wife,' he said humorously, with a smile that changed his whole appearance. 'Excuse me.'

As we drank the delicious coffee, Sarah and David did most of the talking, she asking questions, he supplying the answers in a smiling, indulgent manner. This was a David I had never seen—the affectionate older brother. After a while, Ben rejoined us and sat listening quietly to the banter. It might have been any normal family evening, except that when Ben and David met each other's glance there was in their eyes a coldness that was far from brotherly.

Sarah cleared the cups and announced that she was going to get our rooms ready. When I offered to help, she seemed flustered, but eventually agreed and we left the men together in an atmosphere that was electric.

'It's nice to have another girl in the house,' Sarah chatted as she took sheets and pillowcases from a spacious linen cupboard on the first floor landing and led the way into a pleasant, blue-painted bedroom. 'I think we're going to be friends. It's such a relief. I was terrified we might make a bad impression and David would rush you away in disgust. We aren't very sophisticated, I'm afraid. Not that we couldn't afford to be, but Dad hates show. He was brought up in Newcastle, you know, in a miner's cottage, and he won't have what he calls "airs and graces".'

I glanced down at my fashionable dress and pink-nailed hands, wondering if her father thought I was 'showy'. Perhaps he did. It would account for some of the coolness of his manner.

'I wish David had warned you,' I said. 'He led me to believe that he had. If I'd known . . .'

'Heavens, that doesn't matter. I'm glad you've come. I only hope . . . Here, catch hold of this sheet. It is kind of you to help. I don't suppose you do much housework normally.'

'Not much,' I admitted. 'Not since I left home. But I do know how.'

When the finished bed was covered by its blue spread, I glanced out of the window, which was in the side of the house. There was a lovely view of part of the lake. Beyond a row of bushes lay what was obviously the boat-yard run by Tom Elliott and his younger son—a broad, gravelled area edging on to the water, with several boats, some upside down, waiting patiently for attention. There was also what appeared to be a new boat-house—a two-storey wooden building with frosted windows on the ground floor. The upper window wore gay check curtains, and a model yacht standing on the window-sill was silhouetted by the light inside the room.

Sarah had joined me and was staring at the boat-house with a far-away expression in her brown eyes.

'Does someone live there?' I asked conversationally.

Sarah nodded, her dark hair swinging on to her cheeks. 'Richard Sharp—Ben's mechanic.'

'Mechanic? Oh, I see. He deals with motor-boats, does he?'

She looked round at me, studying my face. 'He does, but . . . Well, they've got a bigger project going. I suppose you'll hear about it eventually. Do you swear not to breathe a word if I tell you?'

I nodded wordlessly, curious to know this secret.

'They're building a speed-boat,' Sarah said, brown eyes sparkling. 'They're going to try for the water speed record. Isn't it thrilling?'

'Marvellous,' I agreed. 'But why the secrecy? Surely . . .'

'Ben's afraid someone might sabotage it. There's a lot of jealousy involved, you know, and the boat's a new shape that Ben has designed. He's very good at that. He could be very successful, if he gave his mind to it. But there's the yard to run and everything, so he can't do as much as he would like. He's got a study in the attic, with a drawing-board. I'll

19

show it to you, if you like, when we've made David's bed. Ben keeps all his models in there, perfect little boats. I love to go and see them. And . . .' She paused, glancing almost guiltily at the door as something thumped on the landing.

Seconds later, the door was shouldered open by Ben, who was carrying my suitcases.

'Oh, I'm sorry,' I gasped. 'I forgot all about them. It's very kind . . .'

'No bother,' Ben said easily, his black eyes fathomless, unsmiling. 'I'm sure Dave would have done it if he'd been able.'

'It's wonderful to have him home, isn't it?' Sarah said, her tone begging agreement. 'And Carole, too.'

Ben inclined his head towards me. 'Miss Davies is very welcome.'

'Carole,' I corrected.

'Carole. Yes, thank you. Well, I'll go and get Dave's luggage, if you ladies will excuse me.'

When he was gone, I turned to Sarah, about to make some remark which died on my lips when I saw the hurt puzzlement on her face.

'Anything wrong?' I asked.

'No. It's just . . . I can't understand what's wrong with Ben. He's not being himself.'

'Is it because David and I have come?'

Sarah looked shocked. 'Oh, no, I don't think . . . Well, perhaps it is. Not you. David. There's always been a . . . well, I suppose you'd call it jealousy, between them. You know how it is with brothers. David's the more attractive. He was always surrounded by girls, but, oh!' she broke off, blushing. 'I'm sorry, I didn't mean . . .'

'I know what you mean,' I said wryly. 'That hasn't changed. But does Ben crave the adulation of females?'

Sarah laughed. 'Far from it. He's too involved with his work, though he does have a girl-friend. But she's not . . .' She shrugged, sighing. 'This isn't getting David's room ready. It's just here, across the landing from yours.'

We were in the middle of making a bed up for David when Ben brought the other cases and dumped them unceremoniously on the floor, with barely a glance at Sarah and I. As he left the room, he closed the door and we heard his footsteps climbing the upper flight of stairs to the attic and immediately coming down again.

'What is he up to?' Sarah queried, shaking out a yellow bedspread. 'I don't understand that brother of mine, Carole. You must tell me what you think goes on in his head—when you know him better, of course.' Having given the coverlet a final smoothing, she straightened up, smiling at me mischievously. 'That'll do, I think. Now let me show you Ben's study. I love taking people there. I'm really very proud of my brothers, you know. They're both clever, in their different ways.'

In the doorway, I hesitated. 'Are you sure

21

Ben won't mind?'

'Why on earth should he?' Sarah exclaimed, already halfway up the stairs. 'Come on. Some of those models are really marvellous. When Ben has children, he . . . That's funny.' Her hand was on the knob of the door at the top of the stairs. She turned it, shook it, rattled it, then looked down at me with a comical expression of astonishment. 'It's locked! But he never locks it.'

'It looks as though he has done now,' I said, feeling uncomfortable. I retraced my steps down to the door of my room, while behind me Sarah sighed in annoyance.

'I don't know what's come over him,' she complained. 'Anybody would think he was a little boy with a secret den. There's nothing in there that anybody would want.'

Embarrassed, and feeling like a sneak, I asked if I might use the bathroom and tidy myself before rejoining the men.

*   *   *

Leaving my room, I glanced up at the darkness looming around the attic door. I was sure that Ben must have heard Sarah offer to show me his study. His brief trip up the stairs was certainly for the purpose of locking the door, to prevent my going in. But why? What was there in that attic room that Ben didn't want me to see?

I told myself that it was none of my business, but I couldn't help being curious.

As I came down the stairs, I saw Sarah standing in the hall, staring at the closed door of the sitting-room, from where I now heard the sound of a heated argument. No words were clear, but all three men's voices were raised and the harsh tone in them was plain enough.

Sarah, sensing my presence, whirled round to look up at me with wide eyes, one hand to her throat.

'Oh, you did give me a start,' she breathed.

Reaching ground level, I indicated the closed door. 'What's going on in there?'

'I couldn't hear,' she said, her pretty face wrinkled by a perplexed frown. 'I didn't like to go in. But now that you're here . . .'

As soon as she touched the doorhandle, the argument stopped, but the atmosphere in the room was alive with all the hard words still floating on the air. Ben and his father both wore grim expressions and avoided looking at us, while David looked pale and tired, despite the bright anger in his eyes.

'You ought to be in bed,' I said, going to him and putting my hand on his shoulder. 'We've had a long journey and you aren't well.'

He moved irritably, pushing me away, grating, 'I'm all right. Don't fuss me.'

A strangled exclamation came from Sarah, who stood in the centre of the room, hands clenched and tears distorting her eyes.

'I won't have it!' she cried. 'Why must you always quarrel? It's five years since David was home and he hasn't been in the house more than ten minutes before you all start again. Why can't we just enjoy being together as a family? It's always the same. Bicker, bicker, bicker. That's why David left in the first place. It's all right for you, but I like to have him here. And now he's brought Carole and I was looking forward to having another girl in the house. But you don't care about me. You'll make them both want to leave and . . .'

Ben had risen from his seat soon after the tumble of words began, but now he reached out and took Sarah by the shoulders, pulling her to him and saying gently, 'Stop it, Sarah. Of course we care about you. And we want Carole and Dave to stay. You know how it is. We fight, and ten minutes later it's forgotten. Don't let it upset you, love.'

'She doesn't understand,' the old man said roughly. 'What does she know about it?'

Ben gave him what appeared to be a warning glance, which puzzled me. Were there things they were keeping from Sarah? What things? And why?

Sarah wrenched herself away from her brother's hands. 'Stop treating me like a child, Ben. I'm sorry, all of you.' Her red-rimmed eyes turned anxiously to me. 'I'm sorry, Carole. Whatever must you think of us? We'll all try

24

and be friends from now on. Won't we?' she added, glancing round at the three men.

'Of course,' David said, coming to his feet in one lithe motion, and directing a taut smile at his sister. 'Poor little Sarah. You never could cope with our fights, could you? But don't worry about Carole. She's used to tiffs, aren't you, darling?'

He turned the smile on me. It seemed to have grown malicious, but that was nothing new. David loved baiting people.

The wheel-chair squeaked a little as Tom Elliott rolled it forward, saying, 'We'll, I'm going to bed, if you're not. Are you coming, Sarah?'

'Yes, Dad.' She obediently took the handles of the chair and helped him through the doorway.

The ensuing silence made my ears tingle. David and Ben still seemed wary, sizing each other up.

'I think I'll go up,' I said. 'It's been a long day.'

David nodded. 'Yes, do. I'll come with you, so don't rush away. I shall need you to help me undress.' He turned his twinkling eyes from me to his brother. 'Because of my hands, you know. It's a good excuse, anyway.'

There was open disgust on Ben's face as he glanced at me. I felt my cheeks flame.

'How have you managed before?' I demanded of David. 'Last night you were on

25

your own.'

'Yes,' he said. 'And it was damned awkward. Will you deny a little help to your fiancé?' He put slight emphasis on the last word, as if to remind me that we were engaged. Perhaps I was being too touchy, I thought. It really didn't matter what Ben thought. Let him assume the worst. It was nothing to me.

We said our goodnights and climbed the stairs together. In David's room, I helped him off with his shirt, shoes and socks. It was the least I could do, after all. I would have done the same for a lame dog.

'The rest I can manage,' David said brusquely. 'Though what you imagine I could do to you with my hands like this, I don't know. I'm hardly in a position to take advantage of you.'

'No,' I said, ashamed of myself. 'I'm sorry, David. I'm tired and edgy. I didn't mean to be unkind.'

His expression softened and he sat down on his bed, pulling me on to his lap, his mouth finding and holding mine. My emotions had been confused, but as always when he kissed me I could think of nothing but his warmth and strength and the fire he kindled in my blood. It was going to be all right, I thought dazedly. If only I could keep feeling like this.

When he released me, I relaxed against him, my fingers caught in his dark hair.

'David . . .' I said tentatively.

'H'm?'

'What was the argument about?'

'Nothing. Just a family quarrel. Ben and I have always fought like cat and dog. It'll pass.'

'Then you don't want to leave?'

He looked down into my eyes, his face intensely serious. 'No, I don't. This is my home and I'm going to stay. There are things I must sort out before I leave . . . Don't you think you'll enjoy it here?'

'I could—if you were always like this. And if you're sure they don't mind my being here.'

'Idiot,' David said fondly, kissing my eyes. 'They will love having you. Especially Sarah. You'll be good for her.'

*   *   *

In my own room, I finished unpacking and looked around for somewhere to hide my cases. A door in the corner promised a spacious cupboard, so I went across and flung it open.

To my embarrassment, it was not a cupboard at all, but a doorway into the adjoining bedroom, where David's brother was stripping off his shirt.

'Oh!' I gasped. 'Oh, I'm sorry. I thought it was a cupboard. I didn't mean to . . .' My voice trailed off. I knew I should have retreated and closed the door, but my motivation had left me and I stood there gaping like a fool, my face

27

hot.

One of Ben's black eyebrows lifted slowly and there was amusement in the dark eyes which regarded me steadily.

'I'm surprised no one warned you,' he said lazily, his voice deep and drawling, laughing at me. Then he pulled open a drawer and extracted a small something which he threw at me. 'Here.'

I missed it and the key clattered to the linoleum, forcing me to step inside the room to retrieve it. Ben watched the performance with an annoying gleam in his eye.

'You'll feel safer with it locked,' he remarked. 'Not that you're in any danger from me.'

'I didn't think I was,' I retorted. 'I didn't ask for the key. It would never have occurred to me.'

'No?' The eyebrow quirked again. 'Have you already decided that I'm a gentleman? How do you know I wouldn't have crept up on you in the night?'

'I'd like to see you try it,' I snorted, thoroughly angry now.

'Would you, indeed?' Ben drawled, a nasty glint in his dark eyes.

He took one step towards me and I fled, pulling the door closed and plunging the key into the lock, turning it. My heart was pounding. For one brief moment I had been terrified. Nothing else could have made me bolt like a startled rabbit. It was a chastening feeling, but I knew that I had asked for it, barging into his room and practically challenging him to make advances. Obviously Ben Elliott was not a man to be toyed with.

I undressed and climbed into bed, still acutely aware of the big, dark man a wall's width away. What kind of man was he? And why had he locked his study?

More questions came to torment me. What was the cause of the antagonism between David and his father and brother? And all those things which Sarah had started to say but never finished . . .

Less than three hours after entering the house, I felt involved, intrigued, and determined to find out more.

CHAPTER THREE

I was honoured with breakfast in bed the following morning. The sun shone brightly through the window as I ate and already there were sounds of work beginning in the boat-yard.

When I was dressed, in holiday gear of slacks and sleeveless top, I knocked on the door of David's room and found him still in bed.

'Aren't you getting up?' I asked.

29

'Not yet. I don't feel too well. I expect I've been doing too much. But don't you bother about it. Go out and explore. I'll probably be down later.'

As I left the room, I had a childish impulse to try the door of the attic study again, but I resisted it. No doubt the door would still be locked and I didn't want to risk being found prying.

The house seemed empty, apart from the kitchen, where I heard Sarah in conversation with another woman I assumed to be Mrs Stone, the daily. I decided not to interrupt them.

Going through a door at the end of the hall opposite to that we had used the previous night, I found myself on the lakeside. The air smelt fresh and clean and the lake stretched smoothly away from a sloping lawn to tree-crowded hills on the far side. There were trees beside the house, too, marching down the hill in untidy ranks to the edge of the water, where a path led away from the house. It offered a pleasant walk, but I was itching to take a closer look at the boat-yard on the opposite side. I made my way along a path of concrete slabs let into the lawn, towards a gate in the hedge, beyond which I could see the boat-house.

I was almost at the gate when I saw a girl coming the other way—a tall, red-haired girl with a face and figure many a film star might have envied. She was wearing a white pants

30

suit that clung lovingly to every curve and when her blue eyes fell on me they sparked with what appeared to be instant dislike.

As soon as she opened her mouth, I knew the feeling was mutual.

'Who are you?' she said coldly, looking me over as if I were a worm.

She was a good three inches taller than I, but my size is compensated for by my determination not to be squashed.

'My name's Carole Davies,' I said. 'Who are you?'

She looked as if the worm had bitten her, but recovered swiftly.

'I'm Moira McRae. Are you a friend of Sarah's?'

'I hope so,' I said. 'Are you?'

She glared even more, saying haughtily, 'Yes, I am. But I came to see Ben.'

'I think he's working,' I told her. 'I didn't see him in the house this morning.'

'Are you staying with them?' she asked in a shocked tone. 'Ben didn't tell me they were expecting . . .'

'We arrived unexpectedly.'

'We?'

'David and I.'

'David . . .?' Her face lit up for a second, then she looked more closely at me and I was astonished to see her deflate before my eyes. 'Oh, I see,' she said dully. 'I thought your face was vaguely familiar. You're the actress

31

David's been going around with.'

It didn't take much imagination to see that here was yet another of David's cast-offs. I began to pity her.

'David and I are engaged,' I said quietly.

She glanced down at my left hand, where the diamond hung heavily and when she again met my gaze her eyes were hard.

'Not before time, if I know anything about David,' she said crisply. 'So you've finally captured him. Well, I wish you joy. Why isn't he with you?'

'He wasn't feeling very well. The accident . . .'

'Accident?' she repeated sharply. 'What accident? Was he hurt?'

'His hands were burned, but he's going to be all right. That's why we came here—to let him recuperate in peace and quiet.'

'I see.' Her face was a mask, showing me nothing of her thoughts or feelings. 'Well, you must excuse me. I have to find Ben.'

She continued on her way towards the house and I opened my mouth to remind her that Ben wasn't there, but changed my mind. It was none of my business, and I didn't know where Ben was.

Poor girl, I thought, walking slowly through the gateway. Even after five years, David's name still made her brighten. What was there about him that could make women forget the way he treated them? No matter what he did, they always came back for more.

I was a victim, too, I reminded myself wryly. I had been convinced that I was over him, but still I capitulated the moment he appeared. At least I had the satisfaction of wearing his ring. That was something. Strangely, though, it was no comfort. I felt no more sure of David now that the diamond glittered on my engagement finger.

For the first time I wondered about the suddenness of his proposal, and I knew that I still had doubts. I looked at the ring, as if it could give me the answers, twisting it on my finger and telling myself firmly that David loved me.

There was a sick feeling in my stomach as I realized I didn't believe in his love, even now. He desired me, yes. Enjoyed my company— probably. But love me? No, I had never thought that. But what other reason could there be for his asking me to marry him? And why on earth had I said 'yes'?

'Penny for them,' said a deep voice.

I looked up to find Ben Elliott watching me, his brown shirt open at the throat, the sleeves rolled up to display rippling muscles on his folded arms. He was rock hard and forbidding, but those fathomless black eyes seemed to gleam with the same grim humour I had seen last night.

'They aren't worth it,' I said.

'They didn't look very happy thoughts,' he

33

remarked. 'Isn't Dave with you?'

'He's staying in bed for a while. I came out for a walk. It's a lovely day.'

'It is,' he agreed. 'But I'm surprised Dave let you roam out on your own with me around.'

'Has he any reason to fear your presence?' I asked evenly.

'Perhaps. You're a lovely woman, Carole. I might enjoy taking you away from Dave. It would make a change. He's spent his life taking from me.'

I stared up at him, disgusted by what seemed to me to be self-pity. 'Why, I do believe you're jealous of him. That's childish.'

'No,' he said, shaking his curly head. 'Not jealous. I just believe that I have rights, too. And this time I'm standing up for them.'

'I don't know what you're talking about,' I said irritably, trying to walk past, but he blocked the way.

'Make him go away,' he said. 'I don't want any trouble, Carole. Just persuade him to leave.'

'I can't do that. He means to stay, and I have no power to change his mind. David goes his own way.'

'Did he tell you why he wants to stay?' Ben asked.

'It's his home, isn't it?' I exclaimed. 'Good grief, does he need reasons to be here? He's ill and he needs a break. Where else should he go but to his home? He won't harm you.'

Ben studied my face for a long moment before saying slowly, 'Perhaps you're right. Perhaps I'm being too jumpy. I hope so.'

'If it's Moira you're worried about . . .' I began.

Ben's eyebrows lifted. 'Moira? Who told you about her?'

'No one. I met her a few minutes ago and gathered she was your girl-friend.'

'You gathered far more than that, if I understand you correctly,' he said, with a smile that died before it really appeared. 'No, it's not Moira. But if he does try to take her back, I have my answer, don't I?'

I shook my head slightly, not following his reasoning.

'I'll take you,' he said, mouth twitching with amusement.

Involuntarily, I stepped back, catching my heel on a big stone, so that I would have fallen if Ben hadn't caught my arm.

'You're afraid of me,' he said wonderingly, his fingers bruising my flesh. 'Why, Carole? Do you think it possible that I could steal you from him? What? Handsome dare-devil Dave? I thought he hypnotized his women.'

'Stop it!' I exclaimed, jerking my arm away and rubbing it vigorously.

'I was only joking,' he said. 'Really, you're the one who ought to be worried about Moira. She used to carry quite a torch. And you know what Dave's like. Or do you?'

'Yes, I do,' I spat. 'I don't need you to tell me.'

'Is that what you were thinking about just now?'

'Is that any of your business?' I returned.

He shrugged his broad shoulders and his dark face was suddenly gloomy. 'Probably not. Would you like to see around the boat-yard?'

'With you?' I said rudely, still smarting.

A smile tugged at the corners of his firm mouth. 'Of course. I promise not to make advances. I'm fully aware that you're wearing Dave's brand.'

Was that what it was? I wondered, turning the ring with my thumb—a sign of possession? Somehow I didn't relish the thought of being owned by David.

Swift steps on the gravel made us both look round. Moira was coming through the gateway, tossing her red curls, a bright smile on her lips.

'I've been looking for you, Ben.'

'I've been here all morning,' he replied. 'You've met Carole, I think.'

'Yes.' Moira dismissed me with a nod and turned to slip her arm through Ben's. 'I'm sorry, dear, but I won't be able to come out tonight after all. I have to be on duty at six. One of the other girls has gone down with measles and I have to fill in for her.'

I was moving away, glad of the reprieve from Ben's presence. He made me feel nervous, though I didn't understand why. It couldn't be only because he was so big and evidently strong. There was something else behind my apprehension, but I couldn't name it.

As I came round the end of the boat-house, a flurry of sea gulls settled, squawking, on the water, to sit bobbing gently just beyond a long jetty where a motor-boat was moored. On the lakeside, two men were patching an upturned rowing boat.

The older of the two, a grizzled, brown-faced man in his fifties, wore a blue woollen pullover, while his companion was stripped to the waist, his thin torso tanned and gleaming.

On the far side of the boat-yard was another building, surrounded by trees. It was a long, low structure with big double doors angled open, allowing me a view of a coolly shaded interior where at least half a dozen men were in the process of moulding fibre-glass shapes. This must be the factory of which David had told me.

I paused uncertainly beside the boat-house, feeling that perhaps I should not trespass further, but as I turned to go back Ben strode round the corner and stood before me, arms akimbo, his mouth twisted into a mocking smile.

'Thought you'd escaped, did you?' he said. 'Not so easily, Carole. Come and meet some of my staff.'

'I didn't want to interrupt them,' I objected.

'But they'll be delighted. It isn't every day they have a chance of meeting a famous actress. Come along.'

He led me towards the two men working on the rowing boat. With his firm hand beneath my elbow I had little choice but to go with him, though his high-handed manner annoyed me. Ben would deny it, but he was a great deal like his brother in that respect.

The older man was introduced to me as Arthur Hemmings, foreman of the boat-yard. He gripped my hand hard and afforded me a quizzical stare from wise grey eyes.

Larry Gordan, the younger workman, was an American and he greeted me more effusively, his eyes boldly roving over me from behind rimless glasses. It was not a pleasant experience and perhaps Ben sensed my discomfort, for he said abruptly:

'You'd better get on with your work before your eyes pop out. You'll be seeing Carole again, I've no doubt.' And he whirled me away, leading me back to where some steps led up to a door in the side of the wooden boat-house, saying, 'You can look over the factory later. There's something more important I want you to see.'

'Must you be such a bully!' I said hotly, wrenching my elbow from his grasp. 'Does it give you a kick to know you can push me around?'

He looked down at me with that maddening

quirk in one eyebrow. 'I thought women liked masterful men.'

'Well, I don't like you!' I snapped, and was instantly annoyed with myself for being so childish.

'Huh!' Ben said genially. 'Just for that, I don't think I'll show you my *pièce de résistance*.'

'Then don't,' I said. 'Get out of my way and I'll go.'

His lips pursed thoughtfully for a second or two, then, before I knew what his intentions were, he took me by the waist and lifted me with ease, placing me on the top step.

'No,' he said. 'I'll show it to you, after all. You may even be impressed.'

He opened the door with a flourish and I stepped inside the boat-house, intending to be unmoved by anything. But I could not stop the gasp of admiration that burst from me at the sight of the streamlined silver shape riding serenely below its surrounding platforms.

'*Aquarius*,' Ben said with pride, closing the door behind us.

It was cool inside the building. Blinding gleams of sunlight came from the lake that was visible beyond the open end of the shed and bright silver reflections danced around the place and played over the enclosed boat. A faint lapping of water only augmented the hushed atmosphere.

'It's beautiful,' I whispered, overawed and not really thinking what I was saying. 'Do you

39

really think it can break the record?'

'Who told you that?' Ben asked sharply.

I glanced round and found him frowning thunderously. Belatedly, I recalled that Sarah had sworn me to secrecy.

'I'm afraid Sarah did. She asked me not to mention it, but I didn't think that included you. Please don't be angry with her. It was my fault.'

He shook his head and swept a hand through his crisp curls. 'It doesn't matter. But we've got to be careful. We caught someone in here trying to take photographs a couple of weeks ago. It may sound silly to you, but there are people who would like to prevent us from trying for the record. There are reputations at stake—mine included—and a great deal of money. So we can't afford to take risks. When we're sure we have a chance, then we'll publicise the project. But for now it's top secret.'

'Then I'm flattered that you felt you could show it to me,' I said sincerely. 'But how do you know I can be trusted?'

He looked into my face with a little frown that cleared as his eyes filled with laughter. 'How do you know you can trust me? I've got you in here, all alone, at my mercy. It's very careless of you.'

'I wish you wouldn't talk like that,' I said walking away from him to where a flight of wooden steps led up to a trapdoor in the ceiling.

'There's no escape up there,' he told me, not moving. 'That's Richard's quarters. He's my mechanic, and he isn't in. The only way out is through this door. Unless you want to swim for it.'

'You don't really think I'm afraid of you, do you?' I said scornfully.

'Yes, I do,' Ben said easily, and laughed. 'You crazy girl, I won't hurt you. But you really must stop giving me openings for that kind of talk. I can't resist it. Are you so provocative with Dave?'

'I didn't intend provoking you,' I said icily, marching back to him. 'Anyway, David doesn't make my nerves jangle like you do.'

'Don't you think he should?' Ben asked seriously, and opened the door for me.

I looked up into his puzzled face, saying, 'I . . .'

'Yes?' he prompted, eyebrows lifted in a pseudo-polite inquiry.

I was tempted to slap his face, or make some juvenile retort, but instead I turned on my heel. The fact that I ran from him is evidence enough of my confusion.

*   *   *

Sarah had made coffee and, as David was still in bed, I took mine up to have it with him. He looked well enough, but complained of aches and pains all over.

41

'Perhaps we should call a doctor,' I suggested.

'Oh, don't be so stupid,' David snapped. 'I was in a car crash. I'm bound to ache. It's simply caught up with me now that I'm relaxing. Leave me alone and I shall be fine.'

'Very well.' I sat down on a chair by the window, looking out through the trees to the lake shining beyond.

'What have you been doing with yourself?' he asked.

'Ben showed me the boat-yard, and I met Arthur Hemmings and Larry Gordan. I also met Ben's girlfriend. Her name's Moira.'

'I know,' said David. 'She came up to see me.' His eyes narrowed as he added defensively, 'Moira and I are old friends. There's nothing wrong in . . .'

'I didn't say I minded,' I said quietly, astonished to find that I cared little whether Moira had been with David.

He relaxed and smiled at me, showing his even white teeth. 'So you've been with Ben, eh? I'm jealous. Did he show you anything special?'

'Only *Aquarius*,' I said casually.

David laughed. 'Oh, that! I suppose he told you they think they can break the water speed record. Did you ever hear anything so ridiculous?'

'Ben takes it very seriously,' I told him.

'He would. Bloody fool. Delusions of

grandeur, that's what he's got. What does the thing look like?'

'It's beautiful,' I said. 'I don't know much about it, but it has the look of a very fast boat. If the engine's powerful enough, they'll do it.'

'He's really convinced you,' David sneered. 'How did he manage that? Did he make love to you?'

I stood up abruptly. 'That's a horrible thing to say, David. Did you make love to Moira?'

'Of course I did, my love. You know what a sucker I am for a pretty girl. And Moira's some chick, isn't she?'

'Yes,' I said coldly. 'Just your type.'

He held out his arms, smiling that seductive smile that women found irresistible. 'Come here, Carole.'

Obediently, I went, and he pulled me down against him, devouring my mouth with kisses. Here we go again, I thought dismally, waiting for the drowning feeling to assail me.

It didn't come. David was kissing me and yet nothing happened inside me. I merely waited patiently for it to be over.

He released my mouth, but kept me tightly clasped to him, which saved him from seeing my face, where I was sure my feelings were written clearly. I half-lay with my cheek against his shoulder, gazing up at the blue sky showing through the window, with the clear knowledge that I did not love David lying cold in my brain.

'Damn these bandages,' he was saying. 'But

it's lucky for you I'm wearing them, or I'd drag you into bed with me here and now. You're driving me crazy.'

'Then let me go,' I said calmly, extricating myself and standing up. 'Finish your coffee and I'll take the cup.'

I didn't know what had happened to change me, but it was plain that David no longer had a hold on me. I knew now that I should have listened to my head telling me it was over when I fled from Lisbon, but I had let pity and the memory of affection overcome me. It was unfortunate that David had chosen that time to propose to me. Now I had the unpleasant task of breaking off the engagement, for break it I must. It meant nothing to either of us.

CHAPTER FOUR

David had elected to remain in bed for the rest of the day and as I was loathe to embark on the confrontation I stayed with Sarah until we had prepared and eaten tea and washed the dishes.

The evil moment could not be further delayed. I made for the stairs, where Ben joined me.

'Going to sit with the invalid?' he inquired.

'I am,' I said. 'Have you any objections?'

'Yes. But it wouldn't do me any good to voice them.'

44

'How right you are,' I said heavily.

As we reached the top of the stairs, Ben caught my arm and pulled me round to face him, saying, 'Will you try and persuade him to leave?'

'Why should I?'

'"Because,"' he said obtusely. 'I can't explain. It's only a feeling that if he stays there'll be trouble. And I'm half afraid it will be me who causes it.'

'Then you'll have to restrain yourself, won't you?' I said.

Ben smiled crookedly and put his curly dark head on one side. 'That isn't easy, with you around.'

'Don't start that again,' I sighed. 'You know very well what I meant.'

'But it would be so easy for me to sweep you into my arms and carry you into my room and . . .'

'You wouldn't do that,' I said calmly.

'Wouldn't I? Why?'

'Because you wouldn't enjoy having your shins kicked and me screaming the house down. I would, you know. And David isn't far away. He wouldn't take kindly to . . .'

'Don't tempt me,' Ben interrupted fiercely, bending over me with a nasty glint in his eye. 'I might enjoy taking him apart.'

I backed away, against the wall, and he straightened up, shaking his head sadly.

'Don't look so worried,' he said. 'I'm talking

nonsense and I know it.'

'But you love to frighten me,' I said, my voice thick. I shook my arm free of his grasp irritably. 'I shall be glad to get away from here.'

'Why? Are you leaving?'

'Just as soon as I can.'

Ben looked perplexed. 'I should be sorry if you did.'

'Oh yes, you'd be sorry to lose your victim, I'm sure. I don't suppose Moira frightens as easily as I do.'

His black eyes widened and I saw mischief dancing in their depths. 'Moira? I've never bothered fighting with her. It didn't seem worth it. But I love to see the look in your eye when I threaten you. I wonder how hard you would resist?'

'If you would get your mind out of the dirt,' I said tartly, 'you might see that I haven't the slightest interest in you and I might be pleased of an excuse to black your eye.'

A low rumble of laughter came from Ben's throat. 'Nobody's forcing you to stand here and talk to me,' he reminded me.

That was true enough, I realized. Why hadn't I walked away as soon as I had the chance?

'I was taught to be polite,' I said, 'even to insufferable brutes like you.' And I whirled on my heel, walking stiff-backed to the door of David's room, with Ben's deep chuckle following me all the way.

'What was going on out there?' David demanded, raising his eyes from a book as I entered. 'Was that Ben you were talking to?'

'Yes.'

'What was he saying that made you go pink?'

'Your brother,' I said, still seething, 'is the most infuriating man it has ever been my misfortune to meet.'

'Poor darling,' David said, smiling and holding out his arms. 'Come and tell David about it.'

'I'd rather not.' I stood holding tightly to the bed end, determined not to get too near him, for fear he should scramble my senses again. 'David, I'm very sorry, but I can't go on being engaged to you.'

His handsome face darkened immediately into a scowl. 'May I ask why not?'

'Because I don't love you.'

'It's a fine time to discover that,' he growled. 'What's made you change your mind?'

'Nothing. I realized long ago that it was over, but I couldn't bring myself to break with you until Lisbon. Then you came home in bandages, and I . . .'

'You were sorry for me,' he finished, and gave a short, humourless laugh. 'You're the first woman who ever offered me pity. The rest are willing to give their bodies, their hearts, their very lives, some of them, but all you can dredge up is pity. Thanks a lot, Carole.'

'I'm very sorry,' I said inadequately. 'But you must see that it would be foolish for us to marry when I . . .'

'Oh, yes, undoubtedly,' David nodded vigorously. 'I agree. If that's the way it is, I don't want you. I only proposed in the hopes you'd let me possess you, if you must know.'

I stared at him, my eyes stinging. 'There's no need to be so horrible, David.'

'I'm being truthful,' he said cruelly. 'All right, we'll call it off. With one proviso.'

'What's that?'

'Save my face for me. Stay here and pretend we're still engaged. This is the first time I ever brought a girl home and if you walk out on me I'll never be allowed to forget it. My family don't think much of me as it is and after all the teasing you've done I think you owe me that much.'

'How long do you intend to stay?' I asked.

'A couple of weeks. Just till I get these bandages off. Then I'll take you back to London and we'll call it quits.'

Two weeks, I thought. It seemed an interminable time, but perhaps I did owe David something. And it couldn't do any harm. Could it?

'All right,' I said dubiously.

'Fine,' David said tersely, picking up his book. 'Now take your stupid face and your pristine virginity out of my sight.'

I left the room, mentally bruised and

wondering what I had ever seen in David.

In the sitting-room, Tom Elliott sat alone in his wheel-chair, listening to classical music on the radio. When I went in, he glanced round and barked:

'Is he all right?'

'David? Yes, I think he's just . . .'

'Lot of damned nonsense,' the old man growled, frowning ferociously. 'Now if he was paralysed like me, he'd have real reason to complain.'

'Is Sarah about?' I asked.

'No. Gone out somewhere. Hush now. I don't like talk when I'm listening to the wireless.'

He swung away, his back to me, his cupped ear about six inches from the radio, while his other hand beat time on the arm of his chair. I waited for five minutes, but he appeared to have forgotten that I was there, so I slipped out to enjoy the cool of the evening.

The lake valley lay deep in blue shadow, only the hilltops still catching the last sunrays, and it was very quiet except for the clatter of crickets and the gentle murmur of the radio from the house. Up in the pale sky floated a half moon that was reflected in the still water and seemed to move with me as I walked along by the lake edge.

Lights were on in Richard Sharp's room above the boat-house and I wondered if Sarah were there. Had I imagined a hint of a romance with the young mechanic? I couldn't imagine her father approving of her being alone with Richard. But probably she was not there at all.

I was so deep in thought that I was startled when a shadow detached itself from the darkness at the side of the boat-house and a nasal male voice bade me, 'Good evening, Miss Davies.'

It was Larry Gordan, the young American who worked in the yard.

'What are you doing here?' I asked sharply.

In the half light, I saw him shrug. 'Just out for a walk, like you. I been workin' late tonight.'

'Oh,' I said, and turned away.

'You alone?' he asked, following me.

I glanced at the house, which suddenly looked far away. 'I was looking for Sarah,' I said.

'She'll be with Richard,' Larry told me. 'They got quite a thing going. Didn't you know?'

'Have you any right to talk about them like that?' I demanded.

'Why not? Say, what's wrong with you, anyhow? Too toffee-nosed to talk to me?'

'It's turning chilly,' I said, increasing my pace. 'Goodnight, Mr Gordan.'

To my relief, I left him behind and soon heard his footsteps moving across the gravel towards the main gates of the boat-yard. I had disliked the man on sight and this evening's brief encounter had not improved my opinion of him. It must have been the contrast with that creepy feeling down my spine that made me so glad to see Ben Elliott step from the lighted doorway of the house.

'Carole?' he said in surprise. 'What are you doing out here? I thought you were still with Dave.'

'I only went to ask how he was,' I lied. 'And your father was busy listening to the radio, so I thought I'd take a walk.'

'I know what you mean,' Ben smiled, nodding towards the window from where the strains of Greig's 'Morning' came softly. 'He's not very communicative at the best of times, but when he's concentrating on music he's positively clam-like.'

He lifted his head to stare at the brightening moon and after a few moments silence quoted softly, 'A pale boat on the darkest blue sea.'

'Who wrote that?' I asked, surprised.

'I did,' Ben said, his voice vibrant with laughter. 'Long ago, when I was a dreamy youth.'

'Is it a poem?' I asked.

'Yes. Maybe I'll let you read it one day. Oh, but you said you were leaving.'

'Not until David does.'

'I see.' He was silent for a moment, staring out across the black lake while a breeze ruffled his curling hair, then he slid his fingers round my left hand, holding it gently. There was no reason for it and I suppose I should have withdrawn my hand, but I was puzzled by the change in him. He seemed so serious, totally unlike the infuriating, bantering man of our previous encounters.

'It's quiet tonight,' he said irrelevantly.

There was a strange shift in the atmosphere, as though the air were alive. I almost expected sparks to light the darkness. It was not what he had said, but the way he stood looking down at me, his expression lost in shadow. I was suddenly very much aware of his hand around mine, holding me so tightly that the diamond was cutting into me. He must have felt the ring, too, for he rubbed his fingers on it and I heard him let out a long, slow breath.

'Perhaps it would be as well if you went in the house,' he said quietly. 'Goodnight, Carole.'

I said goodnight, but my voice came out choked and husky. When he released my hand I turned blindly and hurried away, half afraid of the depth of the whirlpool on whose edge I had felt myself for one brief moment. Half afraid, and half wanting to leap in.

*   *   *

I slept fitfully that night and woke early. As David was breakfasting in bed and Sarah declined my offer of help, I was once again left to fill my time as best I could. I decided to go and see if any interesting work was in progress in the boat-yard.

The morning was cool and cloudy, so I was glad of my long-sleeved dress as I walked down to the gateway in the hedge. Larry Gordan was again working on the rowing-boat, but I only exchanged good mornings with him and walked on to where the weather-beaten foreman was sitting on the jetty.

'Good morning,' I said. 'I hope I'm not disturbing you.'

'Not a bit. I'm only fixing this engine. I can talk and work. Come and sit down.'

He left his seat on the jetty support and stepped down into the red motor-boat that was tied to the jetty.

'David not about yet?' he asked.

'No, not yet.'

'Was he hurt bad?'

'I don't think so. Burns on his hands, and cuts and bruises. He only needs rest.'

'Aye,' Arthur said, turning to bend over the boat's engine. 'He'll survive, that one.'

He seemed prepared for conversation, so I perched on the seat he had vacated, asking, 'Have you known the family long?'

'Forty years. Not much I don't know about the Elliotts. I was there when Tom had his accident, and when Mrs Elliott died. Grand woman, she was. It would break her heart to see what goes on.'

'How do you mean?'

He glanced over his shoulder at me, saying darkly, 'Don't you know?'

'I know there's some bitterness, but I don't know why.'

Arthur sat down in the boat, looking up at me with bright, bird-like eyes. 'You ought to know, before you marry Dave. You've heard the tale of the prodigal son?'

'Yes,' I said, puzzled. That was what David had called himself—the prodigal.

'That's Dave. He was always restless. Five years ago he decided he wanted to take up racing seriously. He'd dabbled a bit in rallies and was getting noticed. So he talked his father into giving him his inheritance and off he went, promising he'd never ask for more. He built his own car, so I'm told. Well, now he's crashed that and come running home. You don't need me to tell you why. Do you blame Ben for being bitter? He's worked hard here and built it up into a nice little business. He's doing well with his designing, too, and now there's *Aquarius* ready to make his name for him. God help Dave if he tries to muscle in.'

'David only came for a holiday,' I said defensively. 'He doesn't need money. He has sponsors.'

'Has he?' Arthur said quietly. 'Aye, maybe you're right. But I've known Dave all his life and I have my doubts. Just keep your eyes open, lass, and we'll see.'

54

His words were prophetic. As I approached the house I heard voices raised in anger. Ben's voice, and David's, and their father's, coming clearly through the open sitting-room window.

'I'm damned if you will,' I heard Ben say, his voice quiet and threatening. 'It'll be over my dead body, Dave.'

CHAPTER FIVE

I shrank back against the wall, for if I walked on I would be seen. I should have turned around and gone away, but I wanted to know the truth.

'It's my right!' David snapped. 'I'm a member of this family, too.'

'Not any more,' Ben snarled. 'You opted out five years ago. Oh, you can come and stay if you must, but I'll see you in hell before I let Dad give you any more money to fritter away.'

There was a sharp thud, as if someone had slammed his fist down on a table, and Tom Elliott said, 'Damn it, it's my money. I'll decide what I do with it.'

'All right,' Ben said, his voice shaking with subdued rage. 'Then I quit. I can make a living with my designing. Let Dave take over the yard and do something to earn his keep for a change.'

'I can't do that,' David said more calmly.

55

'Look, I've had an offer from Ferrari, but they want me to put up half the expense of the car. It need only be a loan . . . But there's Carole, too. How can I marry her without a penny to my name? She's been used to good living. I need your help to make a start, to give her all the things a woman should have. If you refuse me, I'll lose her. Can you live with that?'

I was breathless, appalled, listening to the glib lies pouring from that mouth which had so often kissed mine. I felt unclean suddenly and wanted to scrub myself.

'If Carole loves you,' Ben was saying, 'she won't mind a little hardship. Face it, Dave. You'll never be a great racing driver. You've lived off your charm and your influence up to now, but that's wearing thin, isn't it? So you've come home begging.'

'For my rights!' David flared.

'Shut up, both of you,' the old man growled. 'Let me think . . . Dave, five years ago we agreed you should take your share. It left us struggling, but we came through and now . . . well, maybe there is a bit more which should be yours. But it's not enough. Not half what you're asking. To give you that, I'd have to mortgage the place, and I'm not doing that— not for you or anyone.'

'So you throw me to the dogs,' David said bitterly.

'No. No, there's another way. Like Ben says, you could stay here.' His voice rose

56

triumphantly. 'You can pilot *Aquarius!*'

Complete silence fell, so that I was aware of the breeze sighing in the trees and the birdsongs all around. It seemed a long time before anyone spoke.

Then David said quietly, 'That sounds like a good idea. And if we pull it off, the offers will roll in. For you as well, Ben.'

'*Aquarius* is my baby,' Ben said stubbornly.

Tom gave an irritable exclamation. 'But Dave's got the driving experience! You could work together. That's been my dream. Both of you working to one end, instead of pulling the family apart. What do you say, Ben? Come on, you two, shake on it.' He laughed suddenly. 'That's grand, boys. If only your mother could have lived to see this day.'

So that was settled, I thought, slipping around the back of the house so that I could approach from the woods. I couldn't believe that David would be content to stay here. Perhaps Moira was an added incentive, but I knew David. He loved bright lights, crowds, acclamation, adoration. He would soon tire of Trentismere. That he had acquiesced so readily was a wonder in itself.

And there was Ben, who sounded less than happy about the whole thing. It seemed to me that the old man's gleeful triumph was a trifle premature.

*   *   *

57

As I again approached the door, Ben emerged and gave me a tired smile.

'Been walking again? I wouldn't have thought you were the outdoor type.'

'Which shows how little you know,' I said curtly.

'True,' he agreed. 'But I'm trying to find out more. So you like walking. What do you think of Trentismere?'

I looked around at the lake, over which the sun was beginning to break through clouds. 'I like it very much.'

'That's just as well,' Ben said heavily. 'See you later.'

An odd pang of something like regret went through me as I watched him walk away, moving with an easy, fluid stride towards the boat-yard.

My 'fiancé' and his father were still in the sitting-room, having a discussion that broke up as soon as I appeared. Leaving his seat, David came and put his arm round me and I had the greatest difficulty in not flinching away from him.

'There you are, darling,' he said, so fondly that it almost deceived me. 'I decided I couldn't leave you on your own any longer, so I got up. What have you been doing with yourself?'

He made no mention of his new plans. I was obliged to sit there, under the watchful black

58

eyes of Tom Elliott, and play the fond fiancée. It was the most demanding part I had ever played.

Over lunch, I became involved with Sarah in a discussion of the relative merits of minis, maxis, and midis and the other peculiarities of current fashion. I confessed myself partial to long skirts, especially for evening, which made David remark that it was a pity to cover up pretty legs—a subject on which he was a connoisseur. His father mumbled something about women in his day being the more alluring for being covered up and David laughed, beginning an amicable argument somewhere in the middle of which I met Ben's eyes across the table and felt the whirlpool begin to revolve beneath me again.

It was an odd feeling I had never experienced before, as if somehow I could read his feelings there in the dark light of his eyes. I could have drowned willingly in those hypnotic pools, until I realized that he was probably reading my mind, too. And my thoughts about Ben were too confused to take the chance of having him guess them. I glanced away abruptly and forced my mind to concentrate on the conversation.

David was managing to eat with a fork, though his food had to be cut up for him and the fork looked unsteady in his bandaged hand. I wondered just how bad the burns were, and whether he should have the dressings

59

changed, but probably he knew what was necessary far better than I, who am totally ignorant on medical matters. Besides, I am ashamed to say, I didn't much care. As far as I was concerned, David could look out for himself. The affection I had felt for him had turned to indifference.

*   *   *

When the meal was over, Ben suggested that David might like to see *Aquarius*.

'Good idea,' said David, again throwing an arm round me. 'Can Carole come, too? I don't want to let her out of my sight.'

'She's welcome,' Ben said, face inscrutable.

I had a feeling that David was up to some mischief. He must know that I would prefer to be away from him. Possibly that was the answer—he was determined to make me squirm.

The boat-yard was deserted, as the men had a half-day off on Saturdays, but we found Richard in the boat-house, about to clamber through the raised hatch of *Aquarius*.

David let out a long low whistle of approval which seemed genuine enough, despite his sneering remarks to me about the project.

'Can I see her in action?' he asked.

Ben, who was standing the other side of me, shrugged. 'I suppose you could,' he said doubtfully, 'though we shan't be ready to start

60

proper trials for a few days. I didn't really want her out of the shed before then. There are too many eyes around.'

'Eyes?' David said sharply.

Ben's mouth smiled, but his eyes were hard. 'Perhaps I mean spies. We think someone's out to sabotage us.'

'Who?'

'Rivals, perhaps. There's nothing definite, but Arthur and I both suspect we're being watched.'

'Imagination!' David growled. 'Take her out and let me see how she moves.'

'No, don't!' I exclaimed, and was amazed at myself. But having spoken so precipitately I was forced to explain, as they were both regarding me with surprise. 'Well...' I faltered. 'Suppose Ben's right? If he doesn't want the boat to leave the shed then you should wait. A few days won't kill you.'

'But,' Ben said, with a touch of malice, 'Dave's naturally anxious to see what he's taking on.'

David shot him a look of pure hatred and Ben said apologetically, 'Oh, I'm sorry. Haven't you told Carole you'll be staying here?'

'I hadn't,' David said crisply. 'You might have left that for me to do.'

'Tell me now,' I suggested, as casually as I could. 'Are you really going to stay? But what about your racing, David?'

His lips drew back from his teeth. 'I shall go back to that later. We'll discuss it when we're alone, if you don't mind.' He turned to the door. 'Now I'm going to lie down for an hour.'

As he strode away, Ben touched my shoulder and said very quietly, 'Thank you, Carole.'

'For what?' I asked, turning to look up at him.

'For being on my side about the boat. And I'm sorry if I spoke out of turn. I thought he would have told you.'

'You meant to make trouble,' I chided.

Ben pulled his mouth awry. 'Yes, and I'm . . . No, damn it, I'm not sorry. He should have told you. In his shoes, I would have done. It's your life, too.'

'I shouldn't worry about it,' I said.

'I can't help myself. Are you sure you're going to be happy with Dave?'

I was prompted to tell him that the engagement was off, but across the shed Richard Sharp was an interested spectator, even if he couldn't hear all we said, and I didn't feel able to reveal the truth until David gave me leave.

So I said, 'I think that's my affair, Ben,' and walked away from him, through the door and down the steps.

I passed the rest of the afternoon pleasantly in company with Sarah, as David had again taken to his bed. He reappeared at tea-time, however, but didn't mention the altercation, though occasionally I caught him watching me with a speculative look in his eye, as if wondering what I would do now.

While we ate, Tom questioned Ben about the progress of work on *Aquarius* and in the yard in general, mentioning the motor-boat which Arthur had been repairing.

'It's done,' Ben said. 'I thought I'd take it out tonight to make sure it's O.K. before we send it back.' He glanced around the table. 'Would anyone like to come? Free trips on the *Skylark*. Sarah?'

She shook her head. 'Not me, Ben. I've got a date.'

Ben looked at me and then at David. 'How about you and Carole? There's room.'

'Carole can go if she likes,' David replied, intent on his food. 'Although Moira did say she might come tonight.'

'She didn't tell me so,' Ben said.

'Didn't she?' David's voice was filled with studied unconcern. 'Well, she offered to renew these dressings for me. Perhaps she forgot to mention it to you.'

'Most likely,' Ben said heavily, and his eyes met mine. 'In that case, Carole will be free to come.'

I had been resisting the temptation to accept, but since David was so blatant about Moira . . .

'I'd love to,' I said brightly. 'I've been

wanting to have a good look round the lake.'

The sky was still cloudy and the breeze cool, so I dressed in a pale blue pants suit that looked elegant yet was warm and would preserve my modesty while climbing in and out of the boat.

Sarah accompanied us as far as the boat-house. She was going to spend the evening with Richard again.

'We might go for a drink,' she laughed, 'if Richard can get his motor-bike going.'

'Take care of yourself,' Ben said solemnly. 'You know what I mean.'

She punched him playfully. 'Yes, I know. You mean I'm to behave myself. I might say the same to you, brother dear. It's the wierdest arrangement ever—you going off with your brother's fiancée, while your girl-friend visits your brother. Anybody else would think we were a crazy family.'

'Anybody else can go to the devil,' Ben said, taking my arm and leading me away to where the motor-boat was moored at the jetty.

It was a large, expensive boat with an elegant red prow and perspex windshield to guard the occupants of the slippery, glass-fibre seats. Though hard to the touch, the seats were comfortable, being moulded to fit the body.

Ben cast off the line and sat down beside me, starting the motor with a capable brown hand.

'I hope you don't get sea-sick,' he said.

'Not often,' I replied.

He turned his head and met my eyes in a long, serious glance as he said, 'Shall we take it fast or slow?'

'Is there any hurry?' I said carefully.

Ben smiled briefly. 'None at all.'

The boat moved slowly away, leaving a lazy wake rippling gently behind. A shaft of golden light lay along the water and when we moved into it I saw the sun sinking into a cleft between two hills at the far end of the lake.

'Is this lake long enough for a timed run?' I asked.

Ben shook his head. 'When the trials are finished we're moving to Coniston, if we can get permission. Trentismere's only four miles long. And it's difficult to get close to. That's why it's not so commercialized as the other lakes. We do get a few tourists in Trentismere village, but they're mostly walking enthusiasts—they have to be. There's only the one road. Do you think you'll get bored with it?'

'No.' That was the truth, in two ways—I loved wild, lonely places, and anyway I wasn't staying.

'You sound very sure of it,' Ben said in surprise.

'I am. Ben, don't you mind that Moira was coming to see David?'

'Why should I? She's nothing to me. You're the one who should have objected. Is that why

65

you came? To get back at him?'

'I came because I wanted to,' I said, watching his craggy profile.

'Are you really that sure of Dave?' he asked.

I was twisting the diamond ring round and round on my finger, very tempted to take it off and confine it with a flourish to the depths of Lake Trentismere. It was the symbol of everything I disliked about David.

'Carole?' Ben turned his head to look at me quizzically. 'I said . . .'

'I heard what you said,' I replied thoughtfully. 'I was wondering how to answer you.'

'Try the truth.'

'I'll think about it.'

Frowning, he returned his attention to the boat.

As the sun dropped lower, blue shadows poured into the valley and the water took on the pink glow that was following the sun from the sky. It was an enchanted place, undisturbed by the low mutter of the boat's engine, and I could see no signs of other human life. We might have been the last two people on earth. Or the first two.

When we reached the end of the lake, Ben pulled the boat round against some rocks and, without a word, climbed out and tied the rope to a boulder before coming back and offering me his hand.

'Stretch your legs,' he said. 'Come on. I

won't bite.'

'Is that a promise?' I said, half-seriously, clambering to the swaying side of the boat.

Ben placed his hands around my waist and lifted me from the boat, letting me down slowly against him.

'No,' he said hoarsely. 'I don't promise anything. We both knew we were asking for trouble when we came out together. What the hell are you playing at, Carole? Are you just a man-crazy dolly out for kicks?'

'Is that the way it seems?' I asked, astounded.

'What else can I think?' Ben asked, turning away and distractedly running a hand through his hair.

My head was suddenly clear now. Incredible though it was, I knew what I wanted and what I must do to get it. I shall never know how it happened. All I know is that it did. At that moment and in that place there was nothing else in the world that mattered.

'Ben.'

He looked round and I held up my hand, so that the diamond flashed rainbows in the last ray of sun. 'You see this?'

'I see it.'

'It's not real,' I said. 'What it symbolizes is a fake.'

Ben stared at me dumbly.

'I'm not engaged to David,' I said with deliberation. 'I was, but that was a mistake. If ever I loved him, it is not so now.'

'In these two days?' he said sceptically.

'No. It happened long ago. I was ... disenchanted. But I hadn't completely forgotten how it felt. I finished with him. Walked out. Left him. And that same day he crashed and was hurt. I felt responsible. When he came back I was so glad to see him on his feet that I forgot how cruel he could be. He asked me to marry him. On a wave of pity, I accepted. And then he whisked me to Trentismere before my head was clear ... You must understand about David. He has this power over women. This ... magnetism.'

'I'm aware of that,' Ben said. 'Are you telling me he no longer has that power over you?'

'Yes. This stupid engagement was caused by a moment of weakness on my part and you will never know how much I regret it, or how ashamed I am that I let myself be blinded. Believe me.'

'I fail to see why you're appealing to me,' he said, with cutting sarcasm. 'I would have thought this heart-rending self-accusation should have been played before Dave.'

My eyes were suddenly hot with tears, but I knew I deserved his scorn. The whole thing, put into words, sounded ridiculously feeble. But I wasn't going to let him see how much I was hurt. I straightened my back and turned it on him.

'Will you please take me home?'

68

'No, I won't,' he said roughly, catching my arm and swinging me back to face him. 'I'm still confused. My reasoning mind tells me you're a bitch, but I can't believe it. Tell me. Explain.'

'Explain what?' I cried.

'Why haven't you told Dave? Why are you letting him go on believing . . .'

'But he doesn't,' I interrupted feverishly. 'I thought I made that clear. I told him yesterday that it was all off, and he agreed. But he wanted me to keep up the pretence to save his face. It was only to be for a couple of weeks and then we were leaving. That's why I said it was a fake.'

'And what happens now that he's staying?' Ben demanded.

'I don't know. I haven't had a chance to talk to him. But whatever he says, I can't keep it up any longer. I shall give him his ring back and leave . . . Ben, you're hurting me.'

His fingers relaxed their grip on my arm. The sun went out suddenly and shadow filled the valley to the rim.

'Are you afraid of me?' he asked quietly.

'No. Not now. I don't think you're half as ferocious as you make out.'

'It's my only defence.'

'Defence?' I queried, looking up into his face that was a dark blur against the still-pale sky.

'Against you,' Ben whispered. 'What have

you done to me? Why do I feel weak and helpless when you're near me? Why, Carole?'

'I don't know. But no doubt you'll feel better after I've gone. I'm sorry about all this, Ben.'

He shook his head dazedly. 'You're sorry. You're leaving. Is that all you've got to say? Are you going to deny that something has happened between us? Something that as full-grown male and female we both recognize?'

'What do you want me to say?' I asked, anguished. 'Ben, we've only known each other two days . . . Yes, there's something. But what do you expect me to do about it?'

'Acknowledge it, that's all.'

'I have done,' I said quietly.

'And you'll just go away, back to your swinging world, and forget it?'

'I have to go away. What else can I . . .' My voice broke off, for beyond his shoulder there appeared a red glare, shining out above the trees far down the lake.

'Ben!' I cried, pointing. 'There's a fire!'

He whirled round, took one look, grabbed my hand, and dragged me back to the boat.

CHAPTER SIX

With the boat at full throttle, we roared back down the lake. It can only have taken a few

70

minutes, but it seemed that we rode for hours in tense silence, our eyes fixed on the torch-like flames that we could now see leaping and sparking, reflected brilliantly in the dark water. It was the boat-house. The near-side half of it was a sheet of flame.

As we came nearer, another engine sounded, much louder than ours. *Aquarius* nosed from the boat-house, her silver flanks gleaming redly in the light. Ben threw the motor-boat round to avoid the larger craft and I was flung against the side, bruising my arm and being splashed by spray from the collision of the two washes.

The boat rammed into the jetty and Ben leapt out, shouting at me to tie her up and keep clear of the fire. And then he was gone, sprinting towards the boat-house. Even from where I was, I could feel the heat on my face. Flames shot high above the black bulk of the shed and were now lapping round the end.

Somehow I was out of the boat and tying it up, my hands working independently as I stared fixedly at the glaring scene before me. The roar of *Aquarius'* motor died suddenly and I heard voices shouting instructions. Someone was using a fire extinguisher. I saw the white foam splash and ran to help, running far wide of the burning building. And then I heard a woman's scream.

I stood still, staring in horror at the room above the boat-house. I heard Ben shout

71

hoarsely and he came into sight lunging round the corner, arms up to ward off the heat. Stricken, I watched him tear open the door and plunge inside.

A second later there was a terrifying splintering crash. Sparks danced and whirled madly. A hiss of steam followed. Another crash. The boat-house side was caving in. I think I screamed.

Then I saw David running towards me, his face blackened and gleaming with sweat.

'Carole!' he yelled. 'Where are they? Where's Sarah?'

I pointed at the blazing shell, whose glare lit both our faces, saying thickly, 'In there. Ben went to get her. David, do something!'

'Don't you think I want to?' he shouted, shaking his bound hands helplessly.

With a whoosh, the remaining wall of the boat-house went up in flames. David pushed me away as the fire licked towards us. The heat was so intense that I could feel it drying my skin. And all the time, pieces of the shed fell, sizzling and cracking, into the water. The air was full of smoke and steam and ashes, making my eyes smart and run, my throat choke up. I was clinging to David's arm, shaking him, while my mind screamed his brother's name. Ben had gone in there, through that door that was now just a glowing outline of orange flame. Even as I watched, it collapsed, sending fresh sparks upwards. Then the entire wall creaked, cracked, and fell with a crash and a shush of steam into the rectangle of water. The boat-house was gone.

And Ben. And Sarah.

Tears ran unchecked down my hot cheeks and I shook with sobs I could no longer control. The sense of loss that swept over me made my knees buckle. I sank to the ground, my filthy hands over my face.

Dimly, I was aware that someone else joined us. Moira's voice came to me. She was talking to David, asking him stupid questions about the fire. Then the two of them moved away, leaving me alone.

It was then that the miracle happened. I heard Ben's voice, calling huskily for someone to help him.

I came swiftly to my feet, shouting for David, and ran back to the jetty. There at the lake edge, the last flickering flames showed me Ben, soaked and exhausted, crawling from the water, dragging with him the limp form of his sister.

As I went to help, Richard appeared at my side. He gathered Sarah up in his arms, gasping her name, and carried her to dry ground. Ben started to get up. As he came to his knees, he shook his head groggily and I bent to help him, taking his arm.

'Oh, Ben! Ben. Thank God.'

He flung his head back, glaring at me, and came to his feet, deliberately pushing me away

73

with such force that I slammed back into an upright of the jetty.

'If it hadn't been for you,' he spat breathlessly, 'I would have been here when this happened. Stay away from me.'

*　　　*　　　*

My memory of the next half hour is blurred. I was too numb to think or feel anything. I saw things happening, but nothing penetrated deeply.

I heard bells jangling. A fire-engine screamed into the yard, closely followed by an ambulance. Black-clad firemen started scurrying about, dealing with what remained of the fire.

I saw Sarah being put on a stretcher. All the others grouped round in a little knot, arguing, it seemed. There were policemen there, too.

Sarah was put into an ambulance. Richard went with her and David moved away with Moira. I discovered later that they, too, were going to the hospital, in Moira's car. The ambulance moved away, its lights flickering through the trees. I heard its siren begin to wail as it reached the road.

Footsteps sounded on the jetty behind me and I looked up to see a young constable holding out his hand to me.

'You all right, miss? You'd better come out of the water before you catch your death.'

The firemen were preparing to leave, I saw. Ben was walking towards the house, by the side of a man in a raincoat, who was pushing the wheel-chair with Tom in it. A uniformed policeman was poking about in the blackened, broken shell of the boat-house.

'You'd better get in the house, miss,' said the other constable. 'Sergeant Jones will want to talk to you.'

I nodded and quickened my stride, leaving the smoking ruins behind me and reaching the clearer air near the house. At the end of the lawn, *Aquarius* was a pale, ghostly shape in the moonlight.

The raincoated man looked round as I caught up with the group, and Ben gave me one brief glance.

'This is Miss Davies,' he told the man I assumed to be Sergeant Jones. 'She can't tell you anything. She was with me.' He paused at the dark doorway, helping the wheel-chair through, then glanced back at the policeman. 'Look, sergeant, I just want to have a look at my boat. I won't be long ... And you,' he added, turning to me, 'can make yourself useful. I suppose you know how to make a pot of tea?'

A light switch clicked in the hall and by the glow flooding through the door I saw Ben hurrying away towards his precious *Aquarius*.

Still feeling as though I wasn't really there, I made the tea and took it through to the sitting-

75

room on a tray. Tom Elliott was telling his story to the Detective Sergeant, who was jotting notes on a pad. Having poured them each some tea, I left them to it and went upstairs, my instinct telling me to get clean and dry.

There was water running in the bathroom, both taps full on, so I went to my bedroom to wait, stripping off the ruined blue suit and cleaning my face with make-up remover. My hair was a mess, tangled and grubby, and I caught myself wondering frantically how I could improve it. An actress had to think of her appearance the whole time. But I wasn't an actress. Not here, anyway. I was just a stranger who had made a total nuisance out of herself, and no one cared how I looked, least of all myself.

A few minutes later, the bathroom door opened and I heard Ben moving about in his room. Determined to avoid him if possible, I slipped quietly along the landing and ran a fresh bath. My equilibrium was not helped by the sight of Ben's clothes lying in a soggy heap on the floor, but I didn't touch them until after I had completed my brief bath, when I brushed them aside with one foot to give me more room to get dried and noticed with alarm that his wet shirt was pink with blood.

Hurrying back to my room, I dressed in my utility outfit of navy skirt and white jumper, intending to knock on Ben's door and inquire if he were hurt. Even if he hated me, I could still help him. But as I was tying back my hair, Ben tapped on the communicating door and called my name.

'I'm coming,' I said, knocking over a chair in my haste as I scrambled to unlock the door.

Ben gazed unhappily down at me. He was wearing only a pair of slacks, with one bare arm braced against the door jamb, his hair curling even more tightly with dampness.

'Are you . . .' I began, and didn't need to continue, for I saw the deep cut across his shoulder, still bleeding sullenly. A plaster was stuck haphazardly and ineffectually across it.

'I'm sorry to bother you,' he said, 'but . . .'

'Oh, don't be so stupid!' I cut in. 'Sit down and let me do it.'

He walked tiredly across to his bed and sat down beside the open first-aid box lying there, scissors, bandages and tubes scattered over the coverlet.

'How did you do this?' I asked, ripping off the plaster.

'I don't know. Banged up against something underwater, I think. Sarah fell through with the ceiling and I went after her just as it all caved in. I thought we'd had it.'

'So did I,' I said quietly. 'What happened? Did you swim out to the lake?'

He nodded, wincing as I pulled at his shoulder to get the edges of the cut in position before pressing a piece of lint on to it and quickly applying a long strip of plaster, hoping I was doing the right thing.

'Who would have done it?' he said, clenching his hands.

'Done what?'

'Set fire to the place.'

'You think it was deliberate?' I exclaimed.

'Yes, I do. It wouldn't have caught fire by itself. Someone was out to get *Aquarius*. But it didn't work.'

'The police will find out,' I said, cutting more strips of plaster and fastening them in a criss-cross pattern that looked very amateurish.

'I hope so,' Ben said dully. He lifted his hands and laid them gently on my waist, looking up at me. 'Carole?'

I met his eyes directly. 'Yes?'

'I'm sorry,' he said softly. 'It wasn't your fault. I shouldn't have . . .'

That was all I needed to wreck my carefully preserved detachment. My eyes were suddenly warm with tears and I pulled his head against me, stroking his thick, damp curls.

'It's all right,' I whispered.

Ben's arms fastened tightly around me, holding me as if he would break me in two. When he raised his face, I bent to meet his mouth, softly, tenderly, while inside me great waves of emotion rose and crashed on the shore I had always dreamed of finding some day. Not like it was with David. No, not ever like that. Not being possessed, overwhelmed, but giving of myself, surrendering.

When the real world crashed back into our own personal sphere, I was sitting on Ben's knee, my arms locked tightly round his neck, the warmth of his bare body reaching me through the thin sweater I wore.

'Unfortunately,' he said, 'we shall have to think of other things. Sergeant Jones is probably waiting for us. And Sarah's in hospital. God knows how badly she's hurt . . . But there is one consolation . . .'

'What's that?'

He raised one eyebrow in the wry gesture I was coming to know well. 'You will have to stay now. We need a housekeeper.'

'That's as good an excuse as any,' I smiled, leaving his arms reluctantly and straightening my rumpled sweater. 'How does your shoulder feel now?'

'Sore, but it'll mend. Wait until I get dressed and we'll go down together.'

He pulled on a yellow woollen shirt and sat down to don shoes and socks, while I tidied up the litter of the first-aid box and took it into the bathroom. There were his wet things, too, which couldn't be left on the floor. I put the white things to soak in the bath and hung the rest on a towel rail.

'You look very domestic,' Ben commented, lounging in the doorway, laughing.

'I might surprise you with my capabilities,' I

returned. 'But, Ben, I don't think your father will take kindly to the idea of my taking over.'

'He has no choice. I'm not letting you go back to London, so that's that. And talking of Dad . . . I want to tell him the truth about us.'

'Now?' I said, aghast.

Ben nodded, taking my hand firmly in his. 'Now. I'm a strong believer in telling the truth and shaming the devil. In all things. Dad may be confused by it all, but it's better than us trying to conceal how things are and getting involved with white lies and deception. It only makes trouble.'

I was doubtful, however. The thought of facing that forbidding old man with the news that I had thrown off one son only to capture the other was chilling.

'What will he think of me?' I asked. 'I must seem like a Jezebel.'

'Leave it to me,' Ben said, sounding so sure of himself that I was willing to trust him in anything.

*   *   *

Detective Sergeant Jones had gone by the time Ben and I reached the sitting-room. In his wheel-chair, the old man sat staring into space by the light of a standard lamp in the corner.

'Have you rung the hospital?' he asked.

'No,' Ben said, his voice gentle. 'Do you want me to?'

'Yes, lad, do that. If anything happens to my lass . . .'

My heart went out to the forlorn figure slumped there in that metal chair. All his hardness was gone. He looked lost, lonely, and helpless.

'Shall I make some more tea?' I asked, picking up the tray I had left earlier.

Tom looked across at me, his eyes glazed with weariness. 'Will you? Yes, I could drink some more, thanks.'

While I was in the kitchen, I heard Ben talking on the phone in the hall, but by the time I took the tray through he was back with his father and they both looked brighter.

'Did you find out how she is?' I asked.

'Not as bad as we thought,' Ben said, rising to take the tray from me and place it on a low table by the settee. 'Slight burns on one arm and a cracked bone in her leg. It was damn lucky the room caved in when it did, so she could jump into the water before she was roasted alive.'

'Aye,' said the old man, 'that was quick thinking on her part.'

'But she might have drowned if Ben hadn't gone after her,' I said.

Ben grinned at me affectionately. 'Sit down, Carole, and pour the tea.'

I obeyed meekly and he sat beside me, his hands clasped between his knees, his eyes on the carpet. When I passed the old man his cup,

81

I found him watching me with a beady eye.

'Ben tells me you've offered to help out,' he said. 'Are you up to it?'

'I think so,' I said calmly, inwardly wondering what else Ben had told him.

'She's not marrying Dave,' Ben said, so suddenly that I almost dropped a cup.

Tom glanced sharply from me to his son and back again. 'Why not?'

'She doesn't want to. She never did. He took advantage of her sympathy for him and brought her down here to use her as a lever to your money box.'

'Ben!' I gasped. How did he know that?

He put his hand over mine, regarding me with clear dark eyes. 'It's true, isn't it? You told him yesterday that it was all off, but he persuaded you to pretend. And he still used you as an excuse for needing money when he talked to us this morning.'

'Is this true?' Tom barked.

Ben turned to look at his father, saying nothing, but some message passed between them, for the old man nodded, his mouth twisting.

'Dave never changes,' he said bitterly. 'So what happens now?'

'I don't know what Dave intends to do,' Ben said. 'But Carole's staying here. With me.'

'With you?' The old man sat up abruptly, looking worried. 'Ben, that isn't like you— rushing into things. Why, two days ago . . .'

'Two days ago,' Ben interrupted steadily, 'I was content to work and wait. Then Carole came and the waiting was over. I knew that soon after I met her. Don't ask me how.'

Tom snorted derisively. 'Bowled over by a pretty face! I'm surprised at you, Ben. You were always the sensible one, the steady one.'

Ben glanced at me, raising his eyebrows good-humouredly. 'That's a character reference for you. Shall we ask him how long we ought to wait until we're sure?'

'Bloody cheek!' his father growled. 'You young people . . .'

'Are all the same,' Ben finished for him. 'Calm down, Dad. We aren't planning to elope, but we do know what we're doing . . . What did the police have to say about the fire?'

Tom glared at him for a moment, then sighed, obviously deciding that further argument was useless. 'Not much. They'll let us know if they find anything.'

We talked a while longer, then Ben and I helped his father to bed. He slept in a downstairs room which had been specially converted for him after the accident which crippled him.

The old man was already looking sleepy when we left him and in the hallway Ben suggested that I, too, should go to bed, while he waited up for David.

'And lock that door again,' he added, taking me in his arms, 'just in case I decide I can't do without you.' He bent over me, kissing me with a yearning gentleness that made my blood sing. His warm arms held me close against him and for a long, long, ecstatic aeon we returned to the world we alone shared.

Then the front door opened and David barged in.

'Well, my God!' he breathed, an expression of incredulity spreading over his handsome face. 'This is a fine thing to come home to. My fiancée . . .'

'Not any more,' Ben said quietly.

'Really?' David sneered. 'You always did have a yen for anything that was mine—my looks, my talent, my cars, my women. Can't get them for yourself, can you?'

I hung grimly on to Ben, afraid that he might lose his temper, but he remained surprisingly calm as he watched David.

'I've envied you, yes,' he admitted. 'But not for everything.'

David turned his brown glare on me. 'Of course, you realize why he's doing this, don't you? To get at me. He'll do anything he can to bring me down . . . I know you're an empty-headed piece of fluff, but I thought even you had some pride. He's using you.'

'So were you,' I said angrily, knowing myself safe in the circle of Ben's arms. From there, I could fight dragons.

'Face it, Dave,' Ben said. 'You've lost her. You only wanted her as a trophy and she

84

knows it, so stop pretending. For once in your life try telling the truth.'

David took a deep breath and held it until he was red in the face. 'All right,' he said explosively. 'The truth. I don't give a damn about either of you. Give me what is rightfully mine and I'll go away, out of your life, and never bother you again.'

'I've heard that before,' Ben said. 'You'll have to talk to Dad again.' And he turned his back on David, so that only I saw the handsome face turn a livid white, while his eyes glowed with an awful light that I can only describe as murderous.

CHAPTER SEVEN

I awoke to the sound of steady rain on the window. It was still carly, but as it was a Sunday Mrs Stone would not be coming to help with the work, so I had breakfast to make and a roast dinner to prepare. Doubting my own efficiency, I decided to make an early start.

The house was quiet. Everyone must still be sleeping, which was probably just as well, for I had to acquaint myself with the kitchen before I could do anything, and I began a systematic check of the cupboards, trying to memorize where everything was kept. I was so sure that I was the only one awake that the sound of running footsteps outside made me back up against the table, facing the door.

It was flung open and Ben hurtled in, wearing a damp raincoat. Drops of water glittered in his dark hair and he bent over, brushing the wetness all over the floor.

'You,' I said severely, 'are determined to catch cold, aren't you?'

He straightened, looking surprised, then grinned at me. 'I didn't expect you up yet, but I'm glad you are. Good morning.' He came and took my face between his wet hands and kissed me briefly before stripping off the raincoat.

'Where have you been?' I asked.

'Putting *Aquarius* out of sight.' A spasm of pain crossed his face as he shrugged off the coat.

'Is your shoulder still hurting?' I asked.

'It's a bit stiff. Throw me that towel, will you?'

He took a comb from his pocket and stood before a mirror that was too low and made him stoop to see in it.

My dreams had been full of the fire and twice I had awoken in a sweat, after dreaming that Ben was dead. Now here he stood, tall and strong, very much alive, thank God. I was caught unaware by the feeling that surged up inside me and my hand was trembling as I held it out to him.

'Ben.'

He took one look at my face and came to me, pulling me into his arms. 'What is it, love? What's wrong?'

'I love you, Ben,' I choked, my face buried in the thick warmth of his sweater.

With a muffled exclamation, he put a hand beneath my chin and raised my head, covering my open mouth with his, giving me all the comfort I longed for. I held him as tightly as I could, but it wasn't tight enough, and when he let me up for air I was shaking with sobs.

'What is it?' he asked again, pressing me closer to him. 'Darling, tell me. Please, Carole.'

'Nothing,' I whispered, drying my tears on his sweater. 'I love you, that's all. I can't explain, because the words don't exist. I just love you.'

He held me away from him, smiling down at me. 'Are you always as emotional as this?'

I shook my head. 'I prided myself on my toughness, but where you're concerned I'm like jelly. If I lost you . . .'

'Lost me?' he queried softly. 'Are you worried about what Dave said?'

'David? Why, what . . .? Oh, no, I don't believe that. Though you did once say you would enjoy taking me away from him.'

'That was just talk. Despairing bravado. I didn't take you—he lost you. That's so, isn't it? He lost you long ago?'

'He never had me. You have, though. Heart and soul. I'm only complete when I'm in your arms. So promise me you'll be careful.'

'Careful of what?'

'I don't know. Cold winds. Wet rain . . . fire.'

Ben laughed and kissed the end of my nose. 'I'll be careful.'

Yes, he laughed, and I couldn't tell him of the cold fear deep inside me—a fear for his safety. Was it just reaction after the fire, or the normal worry of a woman deeply in love and feeling protective? Or did I have a subconscious reason for being afraid? I didn't know, so I submerged the fear and made myself ignore it. But it didn't go away.

The rain stopped as we ate breakfast, but dark grey clouds hung lowering over the hills and a fresh breeze riffled the surface of the lake. No one was very talkative. David had adopted an ultra-polite manner which was calculated to insult, and several times I saw Ben glare angrily at him, to no effect.

We were still eating when Detective Sergeant Jones appeared. Ben seemed relieved for the excuse to leave the table and his father asked to be taken along to the boat-yard, where fire investigators were working in company with the police.

Left alone with David, I began to clear the table, aware that he was watching every move.

'Playing it to the hilt, aren't you?' he said eventually. 'What are you really after, Carole?

My brother's money?'

'I wasn't aware that he had any,' I replied.

'Don't give me that!' David snarled. 'You aren't that stupid. I know you, remember. I've seen the types you go around with. Ben isn't in the same class.'

'No,' I said, meeting his eyes, 'he's far, far above the "types" I've known, including you. I had forgotten that men like Ben existed. Decent, honest, trustworthy. But thank heaven there are one or two left in this awful world. And thank heaven I've been fortunate enough to find one. There's nothing you can do about it, David. It's so far above the rat-race world you live in that you could never begin to understand it, let alone have the power to harm it.'

'You're talking like a woman's magazine,' he scoffed. 'In a minute you'll be prating about spiritual love—the meeting of minds. Women love to kid themselves such things exist, but men don't think like that. They're more honest. They admit that all they want is an easy lay. And that's . . .'

I walked away into the kitchen, unwilling to listen to any more of David's vile talk. But he didn't let me escape. He followed me.

'And that's all Ben's after,' he finished. 'You'll be a feather in his cap. Actress from the swinging city. You're the best thing that's come his way yet. And there you are, all gooey-eyed and gasping for it. He'd be a fool not to take

89

you up on it.'

I clenched my hands and swung round to face him. 'You disgust me, David. I won't even bother to argue with you. Go away and leave me alone.'

'And let you go on fooling yourself? No, darling, that wouldn't be fair of me. I'm warning you—the first opportunity he gets, he'll . . .'

I couldn't help myself. I hurled the empty milk saucepan at him. David ducked and the pan hit the doorjamb, clattering noisily to the floor.

'You always were a little spitfire,' he said easily, advancing on me.

Heaven only knows what might have happened next, but at that moment the doorbell rang and David stopped in his tracks, glancing round towards the hall. I took the opportunity to slip past him.

An untidy, middle-aged man stood on the doorstep, hands deep in the pockets of a plastic mac that rustled in the wind.

'I'm sorry to bother you, but I'm . . .' His voice died as he glanced over my shoulder to where David was standing. 'Oh, Mr Elliott! So you *are* here. And this is . . .' He looked me up and down, a triumphant smile lighting his pudgy face. 'Of course. Carole Davies. That's interesting.'

'Who are you?' I demanded.

'Name's Lewis. *Carlisle Herald*. Heard about

the fire. How's the injuries, Mr Elliott? Is it true that you and Miss Davies are engaged?'

David's arm came up swiftly, preventing me from slamming the door in the reporter's face.

'No,' he said sorrowfully. 'It is not true. Miss Davies has broken off our romance.'

'Then what's she doing here?' Lewis inquired.

'I do have a brother,' David said meaningfully. 'You'll find him in the boat-yard, looking at what remains of the boathouse.'

I tugged sharply at the door and it slammed shut. But the damage was done.

Furious, I turned on David. 'You nasty, malicious animal! How dare you? You had no right bringing Ben into this.'

'But think of the publicity, darling. Directors will be screaming for your services after this. You'll be the sex symbol of the seventies. The Elliott brothers fighting tooth and nail over you. Can't you see the headlines?'

I slapped hard at his face, but he parried the blow with his forearm and smiled sadly at me.

'I'm sorry, Carole, but you can't blame me for being bitter. I can't help this temper of mine. And I've been hurt cruelly. Say you forgive me. Let's be friends. If your heart is set on Ben. I swear I won't say any more about it if you'll just let us be friends.'

'Friends?' I breathed. 'After all you've said and done? Don't make me laugh. That "poor old David" line has been used too often to fool me now. You told the truth last night—you don't give a damn about anyone but yourself. And as far as I'm concerned the feeling's mutual.'

'So you hate me,' David said dully.

'No. The opposite of love isn't hate. It's indifference. Complete and utter indifference.'

His shoulders hunched and he walked slowly towards the stairs, a picture of dejection against which I hardened my heart. I didn't know what game he was playing now, but I was convinced that he was putting on a gala performance for my benefit.

*　　*　　*

I had put the roast in the oven and was preparing vegetables, when Ben came in and perched on the edge of the kitchen table.

'I've just had an embarrassing time with a couple of reporters,' he told me. 'What did Dave tell them?'

I explained what had happened, and how, and Ben sighed heavily.

'Well, I did what I could to put them off. Told them that you and I have known each other for some time. They probably guessed I was lying. I'm not very good at that sort of thing. But I couldn't tell them the truth without letting Dave down and he's got troubles enough.'

'He wouldn't have done the same for you,' I

said.

'Maybe not, but that's neither here nor there. If anyone else asks you, remember to say we met in London about a year ago.'

'I hope I shan't be asked,' I said, cutting viciously into a bad potato. 'Did they mention *Aquarius*?'

'No. You may have done me a service there. They were more interested in you than in the fire.'

'Scandalmongers!' I hissed. 'I hate them. No matter where you go, they always sniff you out.'

He slipped from the table, taking the knife from my hands and laying it aside before pulling me into his arms, cradling me tenderly with his lips to my forehead.

'It's been rough, I know. But it won't always be like this. Mrs Stone will be back tomorrow and . . .'

'It isn't the work,' I said, lifting my face. 'Oh, I'm struggling a bit, but that's only because I'm out of practice. No it's David. He was on at me about you and then that damn reporter came and then David went all po-faced and pitiful and begged me to be friends. I don't know whether I'm coming or going . . . But I feel better now you're here,' I added, snuggling against his dear warmth.

'Can the meal wait a few minutes?' Ben asked.

'The vegetables have to be put on in about

half an hour, but they're ready. Why?'

'I've got something to show you,' he said, kissing my eyes and drawing me into the hall, towards the stairs.

When I hesitated, he laughed down at me. 'You must start trusting me, darling. I'm taking you to the study, not my bedroom.'

He half carried me up the two flights of stairs and when we reached the attic door we were both breathless and laughing. With his arm still round me, he unlocked the door, throwing it open with a flourish.

It was a long room with a sloping window set in the roof so that light fell directly on to the angled drawing board and tall stool. One end of the room was littered with the kind of junk a family collects over the years; the other was furnished with heavy old chests and bookcases and battered chairs every surface of which held technical journals and the scattered oddments a man loves to leave around.

'You're untidy,' I commented.

'I am. And in this one room I'm allowed to stay untidy. So don't you try and . . .'

'I wouldn't dare,' I said. 'Besides, I love it the way it is.'

As I looked around, my eye fell on a glass fronted cabinet which contained dozens of model boats made from balsa wood. I walked forward to peer inside and exclaim at the minute detail so perfectly executed.

'Sarah told me about these,' I said. 'Oh,

Ben, they're lovely.'

'When we have children . . .' Ben began, and paused as if waiting for some comment from me.

'When we have children,' I said, levelly, though my heart was pounding so much that I daren't look at him, 'they won't be allowed to touch these boats until they're old enough to appreciate them. Until then, they'll have to be content to gaze in wonder and think how very clever their . . . father . . .'

Ben swung me round and clasped me to him, his mouth hard and demanding on mine, one hand caught in my hair, holding me to him. The things we said to each other then are not for repeating.

'Ben,' I said, when I reluctantly drew away from the wonder of him, 'why do you lock this room?'

He grinned sheepishly, running a hand through his hair. 'Afraid of shadows, I suppose. It was this scare over *Aquarius* that started it—I keep the plans in here, you see. And after we threw that photographer out a few weeks ago, I thought I should keep this door locked. I kept forgetting, though, until you and Dave came. With strangers actually in the house, I . . .'

'Did you think I was a spy?' I exclaimed, laughing.

'We . . . ell . . .'

'You did! You heard Sarah offer to show me your study and you didn't intend to allow any suspicious-looking actress to go nosing round your private domain.'

Ben grinned again. 'That's the gist of it. I didn't really suspect you, but it reminded me to be careful.'

'Well, I hope you'll tell Sarah that. She was very puzzled by it.'

'You can tell her yourself. Come with me to the hospital this afternoon and see her. Richard will probably be there, but I think they allow three visitors.'

'I'd love to,' I said, slipping my hand into his. 'What's happening about Richard? Where's he staying?'

'I offered him the use of the settee, but he said he'd stay with friends in the village. Poor old Richard, he . . .'

'Oh, good heavens, look at the time!' I broke in. 'The lunch will never be ready if I don't run. And darling, don't forget to lock the door.'

*　　　*　　　*

I was shocked when I saw Sarah. Her lovely hair had been cropped as short as a boy's. Her face was pale, marked with harsh red patches, and one bandaged arm lay outside the coverlet.

'I'm sorry about all this,' she said, with a wan smile. 'It was stupid of me. I went back, you see.'

96

'What for?' Ben asked, pulling up a chair for me to sit on.

'A photograph,' Sarah said. 'That one of Richard and me that we had taken at Easter. We only had the one copy. But of course I lost it . . . Don't be angry with me, Ben. I didn't know the fire would move so quickly. And I didn't know I'd be putting you in danger. If I'd known . . .'

'Hush,' Ben soothed, smoothing her forehead. 'It doesn't matter. As long as you get well soon.'

'Is Dad all right?' she asked. 'Who's been getting your meals and . . .'

'Carole has,' Ben said. 'She may put you out of a job.'

Sarah's brown eyes rested with consternation on me. 'Oh, Carole, I'm so sorry. They should have asked Mrs Stone to come in.'

It took us some time to convince her that I was only too pleased to have a useful job. Then Richard arrived with his arms full of gladioli and the rest of the visiting hour was gone in a flash.

When we arrived back at the house, Tom told us that David had gone to meet Moira and would not be back until late that night.

Ben seemed restless. After tea, he asked me to take a walk with him, as he wanted to check on *Aquarius*.

'I'm beginning to think it would be better if we moved her,' he said as we crunched through the dripping bracken in the woods. 'Get her safely installed at Coniston Water, in a proper lock-up shed, and set a guard on her. I thought she'd be safe enough here, with Richard in the room above, but it seems that I underestimated my enemies. They're determined to stop us one way or the other . . . Damn it! It's so petty. Nobody knows yet if we'll even get near the record. What's the matter with them?'

'We don't know that the fire was started deliberately,' I said. 'Surely no one would risk doing murder just to stop you? It may have been an accident.'

He considered that for a moment, then hugged me to him, smiling down into my eyes. 'You may be right. Perhaps I'm chasing shadows again. It must be the size of the thing that's got on my nerves. There's a terrific amount of money involved. And ever since *Aquarius* was completed I've had this queer feeling that something was bound to go wrong.'

'You mustn't worry so,' I said. 'It's bad for you.'

Ben stopped walking and drew me into his arms, pressing warm kisses all over my face. We were far away when the sound reached us—the sound of rustling bracken that made us draw apart and stare up the hill.

'Someone up there,' Ben said quietly. 'Can you see?'

'No. Just the . . . Oh, there! No, he's gone.

98

The trees are so thick. What a place to take a walk. All that bracken . . . Ben?'

He was walking on along the path, bending his head to avoid a low branch, his eyes on the ground. As I went after him, he paused and looked up the hill where a trail of broken bracken marked the walker's passage.

'Now that's odd,' he said thoughtfully. 'Why leave the path? It's a stiff climb to the road.'

'Maybe he saw us and didn't want to interrupt.'

'Maybe.' He didn't sound convinced.

'Anyway, does it matter?' I said. 'Some crazy tourist out walking . . .'

'Yes, but . . .' He turned his head abruptly, staring along the path. 'You wait here, Carole. No,' catching hold of me when I moved, 'stay here, please. *Aquarius* . . .'

Even as he spoke, there was a shattering explosion fifty yards away. Ben threw me to the ground and himself on top of me as the warm blast swept us. Pieces of debris splashed in the lake and spattered into the trees. It rained leaves and branches, and fragments of shining silver.

We lay there until it subsided, Ben cursing softly the whole time. Then he was up and running, with me at his heels.

There, where the lovely trees had overhung a deep pool, the explosion had ripped a ragged hole. The trees were torn and bent, one lying crookedly across the path. And on the water, that still rose and fell, gently bobbed the remains of what had been *Aquarius*.

CHAPTER EIGHT

A grim-faced Detective Sergeant Jones called round the following afternoon and gathered us all into the sitting-room.

'There's no doubt about it,' he said. 'A bomb was planted on the boat. And the fire was a case of arson. Paraffin, like you keep around the boat-yard, was splashed all down one side of the shed. As yet, there's very little to go on, so I want you all to think again. If there's anything—no matter how insignificant it may seem to you—anything at all, I want to know.'

But none of us could add anything and eventually the policeman turned to me.

'Miss Davies, I believe you saw this person in the woods last night?'

'Me?' I said, startled. 'No, only a glimpse, and only of his bottom half. He was wearing dark trousers. That's all I know.'

He nodded. 'It's a pity you didn't walk along there sooner. You might have caught him at it.'

'Or been blown to smithereens,' Ben said tightly. 'Whoever he is, he doesn't give a damn who he hurts. He's a maniac.'

'He's certainly dangerous,' Detective Sergeant Jones admitted.

Ben stood up and strode to the window and back. 'If I get my hands on him . . .'

'Oh, for God's sake!' David interrupted. 'We're all upset about it. All that money gone up in smoke . . .'

'You were insured, weren't you?' The policeman asked.

'Yes, we're insured,' Ben said irritably. 'And if they pay up we can rebuild the boat. But what's the point, with this madman on the loose?'

'We are doing all we can,' Detective Sergeant Jones said. 'But this place is so isolated. Anyone could come and go and not be seen. However, we have one or two leads we're following. We'll find this man.'

'I wish I could believe that,' Ben said. 'I'd rest easier knowing he was behind bars.'

The policeman rose to his feet, thrusting his hands into his pockets. 'You can rest anyway, Mr Elliott. He's finally accomplished what he was after. I don't think he'll be back.'

On that cheering note, he left us.

'I must go, too,' David said. 'I've got an appointment at the hospital.'

'Why?' his father demanded.

'Because Moira thought I ought to. She put clean bandages on, but the dressing itself is stuck fast, so the hospital are going to do it. It's going to be a messy job.'

'Do you want me to take you?' Ben asked tiredly.

David strode towards the door. 'No, thanks. I'm meeting Moira on the top road at three o'clock.'

'You're seeing plenty of her, aren't you?' his father grunted.

'Have you any objection?' David said coldly, and pulled the door shut with his elbow.

Tom's lean face wrinkled in a frown as he swung his chair round. 'Sometimes,' he said heavily, 'I think I've lived too long.'

It had been a hectic day, with that uncomfortable, sultry heat that promises thunder. The men had been in and out all morning and policemen trampled the woods path. A swarm of reporters descended, too, but as I was so busy with the housework they didn't bother me.

Between Mrs Stone and I, the washing had been done and the house tidied through. Now there only remained the ironing and an evening meal to prepare. I must admit that I was feeling very weary, but I thought I was hiding it until Mrs Stone told me to 'run along and have a bath or something. You look done in'.

I was only too glad to obey, though I felt it was very feeble of me to let a little housework tire me so. But it was not only the work. There was mental pressure, too, which everyone was experiencing.

I had a refreshing hot bath, put on a clean dress and fastened my hair in a french pleat, with the result that I looked and felt much better. As I searched my small jewel case for a pair of ear-rings, the sight of the black ring-box reminded me that I had not returned the ring to David. It was much too valuable to leave lying around for long, so I placed the box in a prominent position on the dressing-table, intending to give it to him at the first opportunity.

I stood for a while at the window, from where I could see Ben and Richard clearing the charred remnants of the boat-house. The thin, wiry form of Larry Gordan moved across the yard and I saw Ben turn as if he had been called. Larry stood talking to him, his head cocked on one side so that the sun glinted on his spectacles. Something about the way he stood reminded me vividly of the evening when I had met him by the boat-house. I remembered the uneasy feeling his presence had evoked and I wondered suddenly if he had told the truth when he said he had been working late. And if it wasn't true, then why had he been there? It was something I must discuss with Ben.

*   *   *

The evening meal was delayed, as David was late. We had been waiting for half an hour when he finally arrived, in a nasty, snarling mood, complaining that the attention of the hospital staff had been none too gentle and consequently he felt sick and couldn't eat.

'I could open a tin of soup,' I offered. 'If you have it in a cup, it will be easy to drink.'

He sank into a chair, his face twisted in distaste. 'I don't feel like it. But I suppose I ought to eat something.'

We were having cold meat and salad, so Ben and his father made a start while I heated the soup and put it in a large mug that would be easy for David to hold between his hands. When I took it through, they were discussing the demise of *Aquarius*.

'. . . so you won't need me,' David was saying. He glanced up as I put the soup before him, but didn't offer any thanks. 'You might just as well give me the money and let me go. You'll all be glad to get rid of me, so it'll be worth it.'

'It isn't that easy,' Tom said, staring balefully at his elder son. 'The money's tied up in the business. We don't have much ready cash. Not that much, anyway.'

'What about the insurance?' David demanded.

I saw Ben's head lift as he regarded his brother speculatively. 'If we get it,' he said, emphasising the 'if', 'it won't be for some time yet. And most of that money is mine. I earned it. What have you done with yours?'

'I've lived,' David said. 'Not stagnated like you. And don't be so bloody self-righteous. I've

104

earned plenty. But I've had expenses. I haven't been living off the family.'

'Nobody forced you to leave home,' Ben said angrily. 'You could have stayed and worked in the business. But no, you couldn't wait. You had to have everything at once and now you come crying back for more. And we don't have it.'

'You can raise it,' David growled. 'It's my due. As the oldest son, I . . .'

'Hush up!' his father interrupted. 'I can give you two thousand, Dave. That's my limit and there'll be no more. When I die, the estate will be divided between Ben and Sarah. We agreed that five years ago, I know, but . . . well, things change. Take the two thousand now, or stay and we'll make you a partner. But if you do take it, remember it's the last time.'

'It isn't much,' David said dubiously.

With a suddenness that startled me, Ben leapt to his feet and his chair crashed over. 'It's a damn sight more than you deserve,' he rasped, quivering with anger, his hands clenching convulsively. 'And if you don't leave, I shall.' And he swept out, slamming the door so hard that the wall shook.

Silence descended in a thick cloud through which I could hear my heart thudding. Tom stared at David, who in turn was staring at the untouched mug of soup.

'Well?' the old man said eventually.

David raised his head, a lock of dark wavy

hair falling over one eye. 'Thanks, Dad. I'll take it. I know it's more than some people have. But if I can accept Ferrari's offer, I can make a success of it . . . How soon do you want me to leave?'

'I don't,' Tom said, his eyes bright. 'But you and Ben can't seem to live in peace. Only . . . don't go until your hands are better. This is still my house and I say who stays and who goes.'

David nodded slowly. 'But you don't want to risk losing Ben, do you?'

'That I don't. If he left, I'd have to sell up. I can't run the yard alone and he knows it. He won't leave. It was only talk. He was angry. With cause, too. He's worked hard these five years. I can see his point of view. But you're both my boys and I want to do the best I can for you both, and Sarah.' He sighed heavily, looking down at his gnarled hands. 'It's a thankless job, being a parent. Since your mother died I've realized what a responsibility it is raising children. You know, she always said . . .'

I began to clear the table and left them talking together about happier times.

Ben had gone storming up the stairs and when I had washed the dishes I went to find him. His bedroom was empty, so I climbed the stairs to the attic door and knocked quietly.

'Who's that?' Ben said sharply.

I opened the door and went in, finding him

sitting at his drawing board, a pencil poised in one hand. As I went closer, I saw that he had drawn three similar pictures of men hanging in nooses. Their attitudes were graphic, their expressions horrifying.

'Who's that supposed to be?' I asked quietly. 'David?'

'No. Me. I've been wondering if it hurts much to hang.'

'Don't be childish!' I snapped, frightened.

Ben stared at me expressionlessly for a moment, then, to my relief, relaxed and smiled, holding out his arms. 'Sorry, darling. It's just one of my black moods. Don't let it worry you.'

'You mustn't let yourself get in that condition,' I said, slipping my arms round his neck. 'Money isn't worth worrying about. You have so much to be thankful for. Health. Talent.'

'And you,' he said, kissing me. 'But it's not the money, it's the principle of the thing. This all happened once before, remember. He swore then that he wouldn't ask for more, but here he is, big as life again. Why should I keep working my insides out so that he can live the high life? Let him have the money. I don't care. As long as he doesn't come back in a few years time wanting more ... Did he decide what he's going to do?'

'He accepted the offer, but your father asked him to stay until he's better.'

'I expected that. I know the old man's fond of him and I try not to begrudge him things, but it still makes me mad.'

'You're human,' I said. 'Only a saint would take the kind of treatment you've had from David without a murmur. And thank goodness you aren't a saint.'

He touched his forehead to mine, looking deep into my eyes and laughing softly. 'You're good for me. A real ego booster.'

A few minutes later, I remembered that I had to tell him about my meeting Larry Gordan three evenings before. Ben listened in silence until I finished.

'And what significance has it?' he asked.

'Can't you see? The very next night, someone set fire to the boat-house. Isn't it possible that I disturbed him while he was . . .'

'Larry?' Ben said incredulously. 'It couldn't be Larry.'

'How do you know?'

'I just do. I trust my instincts. Listen, darling, Larry arrived on the doorstep one night last winter. He was cold, hungry, sick and penniless. We took him in, and when he was better I offered him a job in the yard. He was so grateful it was pitiful. And now I've only to ask him to do something and he jumps to it. He's always saying he'd be dead if it weren't for us.'

'How do you know he wasn't a plant?' I demanded.

'A plant? Carole, you're talking like one of your film scripts.'

'And you are too trusting,' I said.

'People respond to trust,' Ben said seriously.

'Some people do. But I've seen too many of the other sort. Nice people like you are easy prey for them. You have to watch out all the time.'

'I don't agree,' Ben said. 'But I'm not going to argue with you. We'll agree to differ. I've always trusted people, and usually I'm right.'

'Usually, perhaps, but not always. What about the times when . . .'

'I love you, Carole,' Ben said, effectively bringing the discussion to an end as he drew me towards him again.

Throughout the evening, thunder muttered along the hills and the occasional flare of lightning stood briefly in the distance. By the time I went to bed, it was so hot that even one sheet was too much covering. I tossed and turned for what seemed like hours, but eventually fell into a dream-filled sleep.

The storm woke me. Thunder crashed right over the house and lightning made a blue square of the window, showing me the curtains blowing wildly. As I leapt out of bed to close the window, the rain began as if heaven's flood gates had opened. A wave of it drenched me before I managed to slam the window down, and then it battered on the glass. Another roll of thunder shook the house. Magnificent sheet lightning glared above all the hills. Like a frightened child, I ran back to bed and curled up beneath the covers.

I tried to force myself to sleep, but remained wide awake, knowing I couldn't settle until the storm abated.

In a moment's respite from the noise, I heard movements in the study overhead and guessed that Ben, too, had been disturbed by the storm. Or perhaps the heat had kept him awake and he had decided to try and work. Whatever his reasons, I thought he might let me sit with him for a while. I needed company.

Slipping into a cotton kaftan, I quietly left my room and climbed the stairs. The noises were more distinct now. It sounded as if he were looking for something.

Without thinking, I opened the door and stepped inside, saying, 'Ben . . .' before I realized the room was in darkness, but for the glow of a torch that suddenly swung and hit me full in the eyes.

Before I had time to even think of screaming, the light went out and a pair of hands clamped round my throat, choking me. I tugged at the wrists and struggled, unable to make a sound. My head started spinning. I felt as though my lungs would burst. In a flash of lightning, I saw the outline of my attacker's head—a black blur against the roof window. Everything went red. The awful pressure came harder on my throat. I felt my arms drop, my

110

knees give way. And then there was nothing.

CHAPTER NINE

I remember rain beating down on the window. Everything was black and my throat was on fire. It was a moment before I recalled what had happened.

Slowly and painfully, I rolled on to my side, reaching for something to pull me up. My fingers felt the edge of the stool, but when I put my weight on it, it toppled over, clapping me smartly over one eye before clattering to the floor with a deafening noise. Dazed, I rolled further, bringing my knees up and attaining a crouching position. I thought I was going to be sick.

Then light flooded the room and I heard Ben say, 'Carole! What...?' He knelt beside me, one arm around me. 'Are you all right? What happened? Oh, God, look at this room. The...' He left me so abruptly that I nearly fell over again.

I raised my head and saw him searching the drawers of a cupboard. Papers were scattered all over the floor and every cupboard was open, contents spilling out.

'The plans!' Ben said in anguish. 'The plans have gone! Oh, hell, hell, hell!' He turned again to me, papers sticking to his bare feet.

'What happened?'

I opened my mouth, but no sound came out. My eyes flooded with hot tears and I lifted my chin, pointed to my throat.

'Carole!' Ben cried, rushing to sweep me up in his arms. 'Oh, darling. I'm sorry. I didn't realize. You're hurt. Who did it? Carole? Oh, darling. Darling!'

I clung to him, sobbing now, and felt him carrying me out and down the stairs into my room, where he laid me carefully on the bed.

'Lie still,' he said, distractedly wiping my face. 'Lie still. Don't move. I'll get you a drink.'

He came back swiftly and helped me sip some water. The first few drops nearly choked me, but after that I was better and able to talk in a whispered croak, telling him my story.

'What is going on?' David demanded grumpily from the doorway. 'All this noise . . .'

'Someone tried to murder Carole,' Ben said. 'And the *Aquarius* plans have been stolen. Look, Dave, stay with her while I phone the police.' He looked down at me, stroking the damp hair from my face. 'I won't be long, darling. Just lie still. I'll be back in a minute.'

As he left the room, David pulled up a chair and sat beside me, his brown eyes clouded.

'How are you feeling? What happened?'

'Strang . . . ulation,' I whispered.

David swore profanely and rubbed my hand with his rough bandages. 'I'm terribly sorry, Carole. What an awful experience for you.' His hair was tousled, his expression almost tender. For a moment I saw the David I had been so fond of. But only for a moment. A picture of Ben filled my mind and I closed my eyes to see it better. I felt as though I was drifting.

'They'll be here in half an hour,' Ben said as he returned. 'We aren't to touch anything till then. You might as well go back to bed, Dave.'

I heard David leave the room and go into his own, then Ben was sitting beside me, touching the throbbing lump above my eye with gentle fingers.

'Shall I call the doctor?' he asked worriedly. 'You look terribly ill.'

I shook my head, holding out a hand which he clasped between his own.

'Is there anything I can do?'

'Stay with me,' I whispered, overcome by a terror of being alone.

For answer, Ben slipped one arm beneath my shoulders and lay down beside me, resting my head against his shoulder, his arms holding me close to the blessed comfort of his body. And, miraculously, I slept.

When next I opened my eyes, Ben was trying to extricate his arm from beneath me.

'I was trying not to wake you,' he said softly. 'I shall have to get dressed before they come. See if you can go back to sleep. And don't worry. I shan't be far away.'

But I couldn't get back to sleep. My throat was sore, my head ached miserably, and with

Ben away from me I kept reliving those terrifying minutes in the study. The house seemed unbearably quiet, despite the rain still pounding on the window.

I heard cars arriving and soon the silence was dispersed by voices and heavy boots on the stairs.

After knocking on my door, Ben came in again, followed by a lanky young man with thick chestnut hair and a worried face. He was introduced as Doctor Munro and he examined my neck and throat, while Ben stood at the end of the bed looking harassed. Eventually I was told to stay in bed until the next day and consume plenty of liquids.

No sooner had the doctor gone than I was visited by Inspector Lane, who looked more like a university don than a policeman and spoke in a soft, unemphatic voice.

'The downstairs window was forced open,' he told Ben and I. 'There's mud on the carpet, as if he came in and then took his shoes off.'

'What about footprints outside?' Ben asked.

The Inspector shook his head. 'Nothing. Too much rain ... That lock on your study door wouldn't have kept out a determined child.'

'I didn't think anyone would go to such lengths,' Ben said defensively. 'If I'd known, I'd have put a stronger lock on, or had the plans kept at the bank. I still can't see the sense in anyone stealing them.'

'But you did think it necessary to lock the door,' Inspector Lane said gently.

'Well ... yes. As a precaution. But I never thought ...' Ben looked down at his clasped hands. 'It's too late now, anyway.'

'I'm afraid it is, Mr Elliott,' the policeman agreed in the same quiet voice before looking down at me with a kindly smile. 'Do you feel up to telling me exactly what happened?'

Ben reached out and took my hand. 'She can't talk very well, I can tell you most of it.' And he did, translating my halting words to him into dramatic description.

When he had finished, the Inspector asked me if I had anything to add. I hadn't. My story was not enlightening.

Left alone again, with dawn raising pale mists against the window, I dozed, hearing men still moving through the house, then fell into a deep and dreamless sleep.

Hours later, I came sharply awake to find Mrs Stone standing over me with a breakfast tray, her pale eyes soft with sympathy.

'I don't know what the world's coming to,' she mourned, helping me to sit up. 'Fires and explosions and now this. Oh, Miss Davies, your poor neck's a mass of bruises! Who'd want to do that? It don't make no sense at all. It's pure wickedness ... There now, Mr Ben told me you couldn't eat anything too solid, so I made you some nice porridge. You put plenty of that honey on it—it's good for your throat.'

115

'You're very kind,' I said, my voice still a croaking echo of its normal self. 'It looks good.'

'Is there anything else you need?' she asked. 'Mr Tom said I was to take good care of you. He wants you to know he's very sorry this should happen while you're in his house. Proper upset he is, poor man. We've always been so peaceful here, and now all this . . .'

'Thank him for me,' I said, 'and tell him I'll be up as soon as I can.'

Mrs Stone put on her stern face. 'You stay right where you are. There's no reason for you to worry about the work. I can stay as long as I'm needed.'

I couldn't eat much of the porridge, but the honey was delicious and, along with two cups of hot coffee, soothed my swollen throat. As I leaned over to put the tray on the floor, loud angry voices came faintly to me and I heard the front door slam. A few minutes later, someone tapped on my door.

In answer to my husky, 'come in', David appeared, his good-looking face set in grim lines.

'Can I talk to you?' he asked.

I nodded. 'Bring that chair over. Was that Ben you were arguing with?'

'As usual,' David grimaced. 'He's in a fine temper this morning.'

'Can you blame him?' I croaked. 'The plans . . .'

'That's just what I want to talk to you about,' David said, hooking his arm round a chair and swinging it close to the bed, seating himself with his elbows on his knees. 'Listen to me, Carole, and try being objective. I've been doing a lot of thinking and I've come to the conclusion there's something queer going on.'

'Clever of you,' I said sarcastically.

David clenched his teeth, glaring at me. 'I mean something other than appears on the surface. You've heard this tale of rivals out to stop Ben. What do you think of it? Doesn't it sound a bit far-fetched? Can you imagine anybody being so scared of a one-horse project like *Aquarius* that they'd go to the lengths of murder?'

'I didn't believe it at first,' I whispered, 'but after all that's happened it must be true. What other explanation is there?'

'That's what I've been wondering about. And I've come to the conclusion there is another explanation, incredible though it may seem.'

'And that is?'

David looked me in the eye. 'Supposing you were Ben. You'd sunk a lot of money in *Aquarius* and your reputation as a designer was at stake. Then suppose, after the initial trials, you realized it wasn't going to work. What would you do?'

'Give up?' I was puzzled, not realizing where David's suppositions were leading.

'Give up?' he repeated disgustedly. 'And have an expensive boat lying around useless? Wouldn't it be better to put around a story that you were being sabotaged and arrange things to look as though outsiders did all the damage?'

The truth of what he was insinuating began to dawn on my incredulous brain. I stared at him dumbly.

'Well?' David barked.

'Are you ... saying ... that Ben ...?' I faltered. 'David, no! That's impossible.'

'Is it? Think about it. How well do you really know Ben? Haven't you noticed how vicious his temper is? Think, Carole! Isn't he capable of doing this?'

'He couldn't,' I said. 'Anyway, he wasn't there when the fire started. He was at the other end of the lake with me.'

'Convenient alibi, weren't you?' David said grimly. 'So maybe he had someone else do it for him. Like Larry Gordan, who thinks the sun shines out of him.'

'No. No, David. Sarah and Richard were in the boat-house. Ben wouldn't risk ...'

'They got out, didn't they? They had time, Sarah could have escaped if she hadn't gone back. And when she was trapped, Ben was quick enough to try and rescue her. Why? Guilty conscience? And then planting the bomb on *Aquarius* would be easy for him. A time-bomb, maybe, so that he could get you

118

out there with him when she blew, and make it look good.'

My head was shaking convulsively. I couldn't believe it. I wouldn't. Yet it sounded so horribly plausible.

'And last night,' David went on inexorably, 'was just stage dressing, to add to the illusion. It's unfortunate you happened to hear him. He had to nearly throttle you to keep his theme going . . . Of course you don't believe it. He's made out he's in love with you, hasn't he? So you don't think he could possibly hurt you. You played right into his hands. He's got you exactly where he wants you—pie-eyed and thinking he's whiter than white. Of course you wouldn't think any wrong of him. But you've got to. Snap out of that stupid infatuation. Forget the way your glands react to him. For God's sake, Carole, use your head!'

'What are you going to do?' I asked, brokenly.

David shook his head, absent-mindedly brushing a stray lock of dark hair away from his eyes. 'I haven't decided yet. But I shan't let him get away with it. It's not only defrauding an insurance company now, it's arson and attempted murder. If I keep my eyes open, he'll give himself away.'

'But it's all over now. *Aquarius* is gone. And the plans. Whoever is doing it has finished what he set out to do.'

'Has he?' David said quietly. 'I wonder. It

119

occurs to me that this whole thing may be just an elaborate build-up.'

'Build-up to what?'

His face was serious, even sad, and his voice was calm as he said the most appalling thing of all. 'Murder. My brother hates me enough to do it. You've seen him, heard him. With me out of the way, his path would be clear. And now he's set the stage, hasn't he? His so-called "rivals" are the obvious villains, and I'm an easy victim.' He held up his hands, looking at the bandages with apparent interest. 'What can I do to defend myself?'

'But there'd be no reason for . . .'

'With a mind as devious as that,' David said, 'he could easily invent a reason. Perhaps I'm meant to uncover some evidence that will make me a threat to the criminals. How should I know how he'll arrange it? Time will tell. And if anything should happen to me, don't hang around. Go straight to the police and tell them everything.'

'You're out of your mind,' I said hoarsely, but my voice shook.

'I only wish I were,' David replied, sighing as he rose to his feet. 'I hope I'm wrong, Carole. I really hope I am. It's not very pleasant to think such things about one's own brother. But you be on your guard, love.'

'It won't be necessary,' I said stubbornly. 'I don't believe a word you've said.'

David nodded slowly, looking weary. 'That's

your prerogative, of course. But, just to be sure, don't try discussing it with Ben. If it isn't true, it will only make him angry. And if it is true, perhaps he'll finish what he started last night. Dare you risk it?'

I put my hands to my throat, unable to think of anything to say. David started to leave, but paused by the dressing table and picked up the ring box between his bound hands.

'Do you want to keep this?'

'No,' I said. 'Take it.'

Any other time, I might have told him scornfully to give the ring to Moira, but the interview and all its implications, on top of the shock I had had, made me feel dazed. I was hardly aware of David's leaving.

His theory was pure nonsense, of course, and even if he believed it himself he had no right to say such things aloud. I dismissed it from my mind.

At least, I tried to dismiss it. It wouldn't go away.

I kept going over everything that had happened, viewing it in this new light. The night we arrived at Trentismere, I had seen Ben staring malignantly at David. It had given me an uneasy feeling, and then, when I walked into his room by mistake, I had been afraid of him. Yes, he had a temper. Several times he had laid hard hands on me, shaken me, threatened . . . But that was natural. He had resented being attracted to me. And when he

121

stopped fighting it he was wonderful. Gentle, tender, kind—that was the real Ben. Or was I letting myself be deluded? I was almost frantic with doubt.

More memories came to taunt me . . . Ben asking me to make David go away. Twice he had asked me. And he had said, 'If he stays, there'll be trouble. And I'm half afraid it will be me who causes it.'

Arthur Hemmings, too, had commented, 'God help Dave if he tries to muscle in.'

And Ben, again, 'I'll see you in hell before I let Dad give you any more money.'

He had admitted that he had black moods. I vividly remembered the three little hanging men he had drawn. Had he told me the truth about who they represented?

I had suspected, as David did, that Larry Gordan was involved in all this trouble, but when I told Ben he had disagreed, talked me out of it. Was there a deeper significance to this than I had thought?

These things went round and round in my brain, but not only these. Interspersed among them were memories of tender moments. Ben's warmth, strength, the way it felt to have him hold me. A few short hours ago I had lain in his arms and been comforted. Could any man be unfeeling enough to behave like that with a woman he had just tried to kill?

The more I thought of it, the more confused and unhappy I became, and beneath it all was the bitter knowledge that either I was doubting a man who truly loved me, or I had been duped like the empty-headed idiot David had called me. Both of these possibilities made me sick at myself.

Consequently, when Ben came into my room I was unable to cope, especially when he stood at the end of the bed, his face hard, his eyes like black ice. When he looked like that, it was possible to believe all that David had said of him.

I didn't know what was wrong with him, but clearly something had happened to upset him. I didn't even know how to ask what it was, so I sat staring at him, knowing that I was afraid— afraid of losing him if not afraid of Ben himself, for I still didn't believe he would harm me.

Neither of us spoke for what seemed like hours, then Ben said tersely, 'I heard.'

'Heard what?' I asked, swallowing painfully.

'I heard what Dave was telling you. Enough to get the gist. And you not saying a word in my defence.'

'I did!' I protested. 'I didn't believe him.'

He leaned over the bed end menacingly. 'Then why do you look so frightened? I wish now I'd stayed to hear it all. But if I hadn't gone away when I did I'd have come in here and killed him . . . I trusted you, Carole. I don't like being betrayed.'

He took two steps towards me.

Involuntarily, I cowered back against the pillows.

Ben stood quite still, his eyes filling with disgust and loathing, his mouth twisting.

'My God!' he got out. 'You can believe that of me. After everything . . .' He turned on his heel.

'Ben!' I said anxiously. 'Ben!'

But he was gone.

*   *   *

When Mrs Stone brought my lunch—soup, followed by jelly and blancmange—she chatted worriedly about 'Mr Ben' being in a filthy temper and not one word from him but he growled, and 'poor Mr Tom' didn't know what was going on and 'Mr David' didn't help any with his sly comments and it would be just as well when he went back to London.

I wasn't hungry. I forced down a couple of spoonfuls of soup and a little jelly, but had no appetite even for that small amount. Mrs Stone tut-tutted over the tray and told me I would make myself really ill if I didn't eat and then what would 'Mr Ben' say? He'd been nearly frantic with worry as it was, and if he knew I hadn't eaten my lunch . . .

'Then don't tell him,' I said, and she took the tray away, leaving me with my miserable thoughts as companions.

I lay down and tried to sleep, but I wasn't

tired enough, The afternoon dragged on.

About three o'clock, Mrs Stone brought me a cup of tea and the news that Ben and David had both gone out somewhere, Ben on unspecified business and David to meet 'that Moira McRae, and she's no better than she ought to be'. Mrs Stone was glad that Moira had got her hooks out of 'Mr Ben', she said, for he was a lot softer than 'Mr David' and would hurt more easily. This opinion did nothing to ease my frame of mind.

She had hardly left the room before she was back again, to ask if I was decent, as I had a visitor. The visitor was Larry Gordan, bearing a gift of yellow roses which Mrs Stone took away to put them in a vase.

'It's very kind of you,' I said in that hoarse croak that was my voice.

Larry's thin shoulders shrugged away my thanks. 'That's O.K. Ben told me you were ill after what happened. You fccling better now?'

'Much better, thank you.' I was wondering what this odd young man wanted, and hoping that Mrs Stone was not far away. I didn't like Larry at all. He had an odd way of looking through me, his eyes large and expressionless behind the glasses.

'He's quite a guy,' he said. 'Ben, I mean. Quite a guy. He saved my life. Did he tell you?'

'He didn't put it quite as melodramatically as that,' I said.

'He wouldn't. But that's how it was. I'd have

125

died if he hadn't taken me in. There's nothing I wouldn't do for that guy.'

I was silent, trying not to wonder if he would go so far as to commit arson out of gratitude. I was sure he would. *If* Ben asked him.

'You had a row with him, didn't you?' Larry said suddenly.

'How did you know that?' I croaked.

'Oh, don't worry. He didn't tell me. I guessed. I just mentioned your name and he clammed up.'

'Is it any of your business?' I asked coldly.

Larry nodded. 'Yes, ma'am. He's my friend. He's upset—I'm upset. So be kind to him, will you? The guy's nuts about you.'

'He doesn't need you to plead his cause,' I said.

Larry shifted his peculiar lop-sided stance, rubbing the lobe of one ear. 'Mebbe not. I took it on myself. I hate to see Ben in a fix.'

'That's very noble of you,' I said, wishing he would go. 'But I'm sure Ben and I can sort out our own troubles.'

He shrugged again, his eyes sliding round the room. 'O.K. I hope you'll be up and around again soon.'

'Thank you.' Knowing that I had been churlish, I added, 'And thank you again for the flowers.'

'You're welcome. See you.'

Mrs Stone brought the roses in a tall jug and put them in the centre of the dressing table, standing back to admire them.

'It was nice of him,' she said, head on one side, arms folded across her ample bosom, 'but I can't take to him. He gives me a creepy feeling.'

I was relieved to know that I was not the only one on whom Larry had that effect.

Another dreary hour went by. I tried to read, but the magazines Mrs Stone had brought me did not hold my interest. Eventually, I heard a car draw up outside. I hoped it would be Ben and that he would come and see me and settle this thing. If he would just hold me and tell me David's accusations were not true ... for he hadn't denied them.

It was Ben, wearing a dark suit and white shirt that made him look very attractive, but his expression was as grim as it had been before, though he seemed less angry.

'Sarah sent her love,' he announced. 'She's coming home tomorrow.'

'Is that where you've been?'

'Where did you think I was? Starting another fire, or planting another bomb?'

I winced painfully. 'Ben, don't.'

'Where did those come from?' he demanded, indicating the roses.

'Larry brought them.'

Ben's eyebrows rose towards his hairline. 'Larry? Have you worked your spell on him, too?'

'He came on your behalf,' I said. 'He was worried about you.'

Ben snorted derisively, then looked me in the eye, challenging me.

'Well?' he snapped. 'What's the verdict, your honour? Guilty or not guilty?'

I wanted him to deny the accusation. I felt justified in asking him to do so. All he had to say was, 'It isn't true,' and I would be free of doubt.

So I said, 'I haven't heard counsel for the defence.' But it was the wrong thing to say.

Ben's face closed up, looking like a totem carving and with about as much warmth and feeling.

'The very fact that you feel the need for me to defend myself,' he said, in a clipped voice totally unlike his usual deep drawl, 'is answer enough. Thank you for your faith in me, Miss Davies. Feel free to leave the house as soon as you're recovered. Tomorrow, perhaps. First thing.'

'Ben!' I cried as he turned away. 'Please, Ben.'

He stood where he was, stiffly to attention, his profile forbidding.

'Please, Ben,' I said again, pleading desperately. 'Can't you understand? I only want to hear you say it's not . . .'

I was interrupted by his father's voice calling hoarsely up the stairs on a note of alarm. Ben tore the door open and was gone, pounding

128

along the landing.

I grabbed my kaftan and flung it round me as I followed.

The front door stood open and Mr Elliott was holding on to the arm of David, who was half collapsed in front of the wheel-chair, with blood seeping from a wound on the side of his head.

'What happened?' Ben demanded, bending to help David to his feet.

'He just staggered in,' Tom said. 'Oh, Dave! Son!'

David's bandages were filthy, I saw, as he raised one hand to his eyes, saying, 'Moira dropped me at the top of the drive. I was coming through the trees when suddenly . . . whammo!'

'Did you see anything?' Ben asked, still holding his brother's elbow.

'No. Not a thing. It was so sudden.' David lifted his head slowly to lock glances with Ben and ask, 'How long have you been home?'

Abruptly, Ben stepped away, his face turning red and then deathly white. He swung round, looking up to where I stood on the stairs.

He said, 'I suppose you think I did this, too.' And he strode out of the door, slamming it behind him.

CHAPTER TEN

Mrs Stone wanted me to go back to bed, but I stayed in the sitting-room, watching and listening as she bathed David's wound while he talked with his father, convincing him that Ben's outburst meant nothing. It was apparent that David didn't intend sharing his theory with anyone but myself.

'Now,' said Mrs Stone, turning from David to me, 'that Doctor Munro told you to stay in bed today, so you just get back there. Look at you. That thin thing wouldn't keep a mouse warm, and you've nothing on your feet.'

Reluctantly, I did as I was bid. There was nothing I could do downstairs, but upstairs waited loneliness and bitter thoughts. My face was wet with tears as I climbed back into bed.

However, I was not alone for long. A pale-faced David came to sit with me.

'Perhaps you'll believe me now,' he said. 'Isn't this exactly what I was afraid of?'

'Ben was in here with me,' I told him. 'He couldn't have . . .'

'How long was he in here? I was out cold for Lord knows how long. He might have . . .'

'No, David!' I put my hands over my ears. 'I won't listen.'

'You little fool!' David said roughly. 'What

did you have to tell him for?'

'I didn't tell him. He heard you talking. Didn't he mention it to you?'

'Not a word. But that's obviously why he belted me. To keep me quiet.'

'Will you tell the police?' I asked.

'I've already called them. I shan't tell them who I suspect, though. If he doesn't come home, he'll incriminate himself.'

'Of course he'll come,' I said wildly. 'He didn't hit you, I'm sure of it. If it had been him, he would have finished the job, not left you alive to tell the tale.'

'Then who did hit me?'

'It must be the people who destroyed *Aquarius*. Perhaps they thought you were Ben and . . .' I clapped my hands to my mouth as a terrifying idea came to me. 'David!' I wailed. 'They're after him now. They blew up the boat, stole the plans, but Ben . . . Ben could design another boat. So they're trying to kill him. Oh, David! David! We've got to warn him. Where will he have gone?'

'How the hell should I know? Probably gone to drive over a cliff. He was mad enough.'

'Don't!' I choked. 'Oh, no, David. If he did that it would be my fault. I doubted him. He must come back. We've got to tell him, warn him. I've got to make him believe in me again. Can't you try and find him?'

'How? Follow that damn great Rover on my two feet? I might stand a chance if I could use

131

the Mistrale, but which way did he go? To the village? To Carlisle? Into the hills?'

I put my head down in my hands, weeping soundlessly, hopelessly. Why hadn't I made things right when I had the chance?

I felt David stroke my hair. 'Don't cry, Carole. I'm sorry I brought you into this, but I still think Ben's the obvious answer.'

I sat up, flinging his hands away from me. 'Then why didn't he kill you when he had the chance? That's what you said he would do. It wasn't Ben. Somebody else hit you. And I wish they'd done a better job. Then you wouldn't be here saying such awful things about Ben.'

Affronted, David stepped away, his lips curling. 'All right, then. If that's the way you feel . . . And if you're murdered in your sleep, don't say I didn't warn you.'

A hiccough of laughter jolted me. And another. Soon I was laughing loudly, making such a terrible sound that I was frightened into stopping it. David looked down at me with a peculiar expression on his face.

'The sooner you get back to London, the better,' he said as he left me.

I lay down and closed my eyes again. By the time I had managed to calm myself completely, Mrs Stone was coming in with more food I couldn't eat.

No, she said in answer to my question, 'Mr Ben' wasn't home yet.

During the evening, I had a bath and

washed my hair, an operation which took much time and trouble since my neck was almost too stiff to bend. But my morale was lifted by the very normalcy of the task.

The bruises around my throat had turned a sickly purplish black which almost matched the clean lace nightdress I put on, and there was another bruise over my right eyebrow, where the stool had hit me. The rest of my face was unnaturally pale and my eyes looked too big, their colour dulled. Staring in the mirror did me no good at all.

Mrs Stone, when she brought me a cup of hot milk sweetened with honey, was appalled to see my wet hair.

'You shouldn't have done that alone,' she chided. 'I was here. Why didn't you ask me?'

'You've done quite enough,' I told her. 'But tomorrow I shall be up to help you.'

'We'll see about that,' she said, nodding wisely at me.

'Is Ben home?' I asked, though I knew very well I would have heard the car if he had come.

He wasn't, she said, so she had phoned for a taxi. 'Mr Ben' had been going to give her a lift. But in all the hoo-hah it was no wonder he'd forgotten. And 'Mr Tom' wasn't at all pleased, as she'd had to help him to bed and the silly man had been embarrassed, as if she'd never seen a man before and her a married woman for thirty years.

'I'll come as soon as I can in the morning,'

she concluded. 'You're not to worry about a thing till I get here. They'll wait for their breakfasts for once. Now you take care of yourself, Miss Carole. I hope you won't feel so poorly tomorrow. Goodnight.'

I smiled to myself as she went out. I had graduated from 'Miss Davies' to 'Miss Carole', so she must have accepted me.

But the humour didn't linger. Ben wasn't home. So where was he?

I sat thinking about it while I sipped my drink, which had rum in it as well as honey. If I were asleep when he came in, I must somehow let him know that I wanted to apologize. The only thing I could think of was a note, pinned to his side of the connecting door and saying, 'This door is not locked. I love you, Ben.' I hoped he would understand.

I hadn't expected to sleep, but there must have been a lot of rum in the milk, for I remember nothing after settling down in bed.

*   *   *

When I woke, it was full daylight. The birds sang noisily. The sun was bright in a cloudless sky and my throat felt less swollen. My first thought was for Ben. What had he thought of my note?

Slipping on my kaftan, I went to the door, opening it quietly in case Ben was still asleep. But I needn't have bothered. The bedroom was empty, the bed neatly made, with Ben's pyjamas folded exactly as they had been the previous day. Ben hadn't been home.

My note looked silly in the light of day, so I tore it down, screwed it up, and threw it into a corner, annoyed with myself and acutely worried about Ben. Something awful had happened to him, I was sure. It wasn't like him to stay out all night. But how did I know what he was like? I had only known him five days.

'I just know,' I told myself angrily as I dressed. I wasn't going to question my feelings any more. I was sure of Ben. I loved him and I had been stupid ever to doubt him.

As I went down the stairs, I heard Tom moving in his room and went in to help him dress and get into his chair.

'Thank goodness!' was his greeting. 'I was trying to do it alone, before Mrs Stone came in. She's kind enough, but she's not family. It's embarrassing for a man.'

'Am I family?' I asked, finding my voice back to normal apart from a lingering huskiness.

'You're Ben's girl, aren't you? Aren't you?' he repeated, thrusting his face closer to mine.

'Yes, I am.'

'What was all that last night? Did you have a fight?'

'I'm afraid so.'

'Huh! Well, that's normal enough. What time did he get in?'

'He didn't come home,' I said quietly.

135

Tom was silent for a while, watching me through narrowed eyes. 'Then where is he?'

'I wish I knew.'

'Not come home,' he said to himself, shaking his head. 'That was Dave's trick, not Ben's. Where the devil can he have gone?'

'I'll start breakfast,' I said, and fled to the kitchen. But I had hardly reached it when the telephone shrilled in the hall and I raced back to answer it, almost shouting, 'Hello?'

'Oh,' a woman's voice said flatly. 'Is that Miss Davies?'

'Yes. Who's that?'

'This is Moira McRae,' she said, more crisply. 'How is Dave?'

'Dave?' I hadn't given him a thought. 'Oh, he's all right. I think. He's still in bed.'

The wheel-chair rolled into the hall and Tom said sharply, 'Who is it?'

As I turned to tell him, David came down the stairs, so I handed the phone to him and returned to the kitchen. I had been sure the call would be from Ben. When it wasn't, I felt miserable and more concerned than ever for his safety.

It was not yet nine o'clock, but already the day was hot. I opened the kitchen windows wide and propped the door open so that the breeze could come through. Bacon sizzled merrily in the pan, its aroma making me hungry for the first time in twenty-four hours.

Then Mrs Stone arrived and forcibly

removed me from the kitchen, saying that I was going to take it easy if she had to tie me down. I couldn't make her understand that I would rather have work to do than sit idle and think. She was trying to be kind.

All through breakfast, Tom kept looking at his watch and wondering aloud where Ben had got to.

'If he doesn't come soon,' he said eventually, 'I shall phone the police.'

'He's big enough to take care of himself,' David said. 'A grown-up has to be missing several days before the police are interested.'

Tom fixed him with bright dark eyes. 'Aye. Could be you're right. But after the goings-on here . . . I'm worried about the lad.'

Mrs Stone again refused help with the dishes. She took the tea-cloth from me and pushed me towards the door, telling me that fresh air would do me good. I wandered down the lawn to the water's edge and stood gazing dismally across the sparkling lake.

The sound of a car coming down the drive made me run past David and around the house. But it wasn't Ben's car. It was a taxi. And in it were Sarah and Richard.

The fair-haired young man leapt from the vehicle and bent to assist Sarah. Her left leg was heavily strapped and there was still a light dressing on her burned arm, but her face, despite the ugly pink patches that hadn't yet faded, was glowing as she looked up at the

137

house.

'Oh,' she breathed, 'it is good to be home. Hello, Carole. Are you . . .?' Her voice broke off as her eyes rested on my throat, widening with horror. 'What happened to you?'

'It's a long story,' I said easily, the huskiness still evident in my voice. 'Let's go inside.'

It was not until conversation began to flow coherently that I realized Sarah had been kept in ignorance of everything that had happened since the fire. But now she was home it was impossible to keep anything from her. She asked pertinent questions and pounced on every evasive answer until she had drawn the truth from one or another of us. It left her ashen and tense, her hands smoothing nervously at her skirt.

'I can't believe it,' she said eventually. 'These things don't happen to people like us. It's awful. No wonder Ben was in such a state when he came to see me yesterday. Where is he?'

An uneasy silence hung over us all and I, for one, didn't dare meet Sarah's eyes.

'Where is he?' she demanded. 'Tell me! Has something happened to him?'

'No, lass, no,' Tom said, stretching out a hand to touch her shoulder. 'He was upset and he didn't come home last night. But he'll be back soon, you'll see. He was just upset.'

'Why?' Sarah wanted to know.

'Well . . .' Tom's eyes turned pleadingly to

138

me, but it was David who replied.

'He had a row with Carole, that's all. Went off in a huff and hasn't been home since.'

'With Carole?' Sarah cried, turning to me. 'What did you say to him? You had no right! All this trouble and now you ... oh, I wish you'd never come. I knew something was going on when Ben told me the engagement was off. Why are you still here? Hadn't you the decency to go away? Why didn't you leave Ben alone?'

Tom had been trying to stop her, but she had shrugged him off. Now his voice came quietly.

'Sarah, you don't know. Don't blame Carole. You know what a temper Ben's got. It was nothing but a tiff.'

Her eyes came back to me, glistening and filled with hatred. 'Was it? You tell me, Carole Davics. Tell me the truth. Did you hurt my brother enough to make him stay away? If you did, I'll never forgive you.'

I was on the verge of tears myself, but Sarah deserved an honest answer.

'Yes,' I said. 'It was my fault.'

She gave a strangled cry and thumped her fists down on the settee.

'Stop that!' Tom said sharply, with that authority of which he was capable when the occasion demanded. 'It's not your concern. You've no business talking to Carole like that. Don't you ever quarrel with Richard?'

'He's never stayed away all night,' Sarah said sullenly.

Tom grunted. 'Well, he's different from Ben. And I might tell you, my girl, that once I stopped away two whole days after a fight with your mother. So calm down. There's been quite enough trouble without you adding to it.'

His words quietened Sarah, but the look in her eyes whenever they fell on me told me she was a long way from forgiving me.

Lunchtime came and went and there was still no word from Ben. I toyed with the idea of phoning Carlisle to ask about train times, but I couldn't arrange to leave until I knew what had happened to the man I loved. The house seemed unfriendly now that Sarah was there with her accusing eyes. I didn't need her to remind me how badly I had behaved ever since arriving in Trentismere. I couldn't relax.

Seeing David set out for another date with the glamorous Moira made me decide that I, too, might escape for an hour or so. The cool shade of the woods beckoned and I told Mrs Stone I was going for a walk.

The day was baking hot, but it was pleasant beneath the trees. I walked slowly along by the lake, reliving things that had happened to me on that path. Here Ben had kissed me. And here was the destruction wreaked by the bomb.

Beyond that point, the path was almost invisible beneath the ubiquitous bracken, but the growth didn't prevent my moving on. I was

140

climbing now, up a bank that dropped sheer down to the lake, and soon I was in sight of the road, towards which I made my way.

Across the road, the woods continued, rising up a hillside until the trees petered out and there was only the brown and green of bracken making a thick carpet right to the hill-top. I continued the climb, though it made me hot and sticky, and by the time I reached the summit I was glad to sit down and admire the view of the lake basin.

I had been sitting there for several minutes, enjoying the breeze in my hair, when I heard a man and woman laughing together. The sound came from behind and below me. Curious, I stretched out to see beyond the hilltop and there beneath me was a sheltered hollow where the sun poured down upon a couple lying on a plaid blanket.

Feeling sick, I drew back and stood up, staring back down the hill. I no longer needed to wonder about the relationship between David and Moira. I had seen for myself that they were lovers.

The sight of them lying together in complete abandon stayed with me all the way back along the road, but when I was halfway down the drive it was dismissed from my mind by the far more pleasant sight of Ben's black Rover standing before the house.

Weak from relief, I ran the rest of the way and almost bumped into Larry Gordan.

'Steady on!' he cried, moving out of the way. 'Boy, am I glad to see you. You've got them all worried sick. Where've you been?'

'Walking,' I said tersely.

'Hot day for it. You better go ahead and let 'em see you're all of a piece.'

At the door, I paused, uncertain of my reception. Ben was still angry with me. Sarah, too. Tom seemed to be on my side, though I had caused nothing but trouble and he would no doubt be relieved to see me go. And David and Moira would be delighted by my departure.

I walked into the house with a speech prepared and a carefully arranged non-committal expression on my face.

They were in the lounge—Tom, Sarah, and Ben, who came to his feet as I went in. He was safe. Safe.

'I'm very glad you're all right,' I said, unable to keep the tremor from my voice, my eyes fixed on a point beyond his shoulder. 'But I think it would be best for everyone if I went away. Do you know what time the trains leave?'

CHAPTER ELEVEN

Ben strode across the room and fastened his hands on my shoulders. When I looked up at him, the pain in his eyes reached me like a physical blow.

'Forgive me,' he said, astoundingly. 'Forgive me.'

I blinked back sudden tears, choking, 'But it was my fault. I'm the one who should...' There were no more words. There was nothing but Ben, his mouth on mine, his arms around me, his body hard against me. He was home. So was I.

Vaguely, I heard Tom clear his throat. He did it three times before Ben let me go.

'Where have you been?' he demanded, shaking me. 'You've been gone nearly three hours.'

'I was walking,' I said, half laughing, half crying from pure joy. 'And where have you been? We've all been frantic.'

'I went to Carlisle,' he said, searching my face as if he would memorise every pore. 'I got blind, stinking, paralytic drunk. And somewhere along the way I must have cried on the landlord's shoulder, because when he finally got me sobered up this morning he told me not to be such a bloody fool. He told me to come home and tell you that ... what you thought ... wasn't true. And that I love you. And that if ever you dare doubt me again I'll put you over my knee and paddle your behind till you can't sit down.'

'He told you all that?' I queried, my voice breaking with tearful laughter.

Ben grinned. 'Well, no. Most of it I thought up for myself, on the way home. And then you weren't here and I thought, My God, if . . .' He stopped talking and glanced round at his father and sister as if he had just remembered we had an audience.

Tom's face was a study of delight. Even his wrinkles seemed to be smiling. And Sarah's eyes were brimming, her mouth curving softly.

'The rest is private,' Ben said, his arm tucked around my waist. 'So if you'll excuse us . . .' And he swung me round, leading me out into the hot sunlight, towards the path where I had wandered dismally only a short time before.

'I didn't believe David,' I said. 'Really I didn't.'

Ben looked down at me, his dark eyes bright with love. 'You weren't well. You were emotionally disturbed and David added to it. I don't blame you for having doubts. I thought some pretty terrible things about you and him yesterday, things I didn't really believe, but I kept reminding myself I didn't know you well enough to tell. It must have been the same for you. And all you asked was for me to deny the accusation. But I was too proud. I wanted you to trust me blindly, unquestioningly. And I was wrong. I know that now. And I ask you very humbly to forgive me for my pride and for the way I hurt you. I shouldn't have left you alone in the house with no one to protect you, especially after what you'd been through. I didn't realize until this morning that if anything else happened I wouldn't be there. And then when you weren't in the house, I was afraid that my stupidity had kept me away too long and I'd lost you. And if that had happened I think I'd have died.'

After that speech, there was nothing I could do but reach up to slip my arms around his neck and tell him everything that was in my heart.

* * *

A long time later, we walked on along the path, sunlight dappling our faces through the trees, our hands tightly locked each in other. We were silent, because we had said all the words and what remained could only be expressed by a glance or a touch. Only when we came to the stream did we pause, watching the water flow into the lake, and remember that we were not alone in the world, that there were people and things outside ourselves and beyond our control, but still able to affect us.

We talked about David.

'What are you going to do?' I asked. 'You can't let him go on thinking . . .'

'Does he?' Ben said. 'Does he really believe it? That was something else I had a chance to think about.'

'Why else would he tell me?'

Ben looked down at the stream, saying slowly, 'I think he was trying to get you away from me. He's been doing it all the time. This is just his latest effort.' Smiling dark eyes rested on me. 'He almost succeeded, too.'

'He has been on at me to leave,' I admitted. 'He said he was concerned for my safety. I'm sure he doesn't want me for himself.'

Ben's eyebrow lifted crookedly. 'No? I find that hard to believe. But he certainly wouldn't enjoy losing you to me. It's bad for his ego. So he concocted this story. And he nearly convinced you.'

I rested my head on his arm, ashamed, saying again, 'I'm sorry, darling.'

'All that is over,' Ben said softly, touching my hair. 'Stop worrying about it. And as for Dave . . . I gave up bothering what he thought of me years ago. I was only angry because he was getting at you.'

A cloud came over the sun. It was only a small cloud and its shadow soon drifted away from us, but I was left with a chill feeling that made me creep closer to Ben's side.

'I'm afraid,' I said. 'Afraid for you. I've had this funny feeling that you were in danger, and I'm sure that whoever attacked David was after you.'

'Why?' Ben asked, his firm mouth lifting in a smile.

'Because you designed *Aquarius*. Without you, there could never be another *Aquarius*

146

now that the plans have gone.'

'That's crazy. I'm no harm to anyone. Don't let this thing get on your nerves, darling.'

'Then who attacked David? And why?' I demanded.

'One of his ex-girl friends?'

'Don't laugh at me, Ben. I'm serious. Everything else has had reason behind it, or seemed to. But this . . . Why David? Unless they mistook him for you?'

Ben shook his head, running his fingers through his thick curls. 'I don't know. I'm no Sherlock Holmes. And you mustn't worry about it. Let the police handle it. It's their job.'

'Well, they don't seem to be making much headway, do they? What if someone is out to kill you? You should be careful.'

'I will be,' Ben assured me with a tender smile. 'I have so much to live for now.'

But I don't think he really believed he was in any danger.

For the rest of that day, life was quiet and normal. Day drifted into warm evening and the scent of the honeysuckle outside the sitting-room window was so strong it was sickly. The moon and the stars came out and the house by the lake slept peacefully through the dawn of a new day, which promised to be hotter than its predecessor.

Late in the afternoon, Ben and I set out in the Rover to have a quiet dinner together at a lonely Hotel in the hills. It was the first chance we had had to be alone together for any length of time and we were both in high spirits as we drove into the lovely wild countryside where shadows were lengthening between craggy hills.

The road dipped and climbed, each summit affording a different view of breathtaking grandeur. In places, the bare rock jutted in weird shapes. Sheep dotted all the hills and miles of stone walls marched in geometric patterns over the grassy slopes, making me exclaim constantly at the savage beauty of Ben's home county. He smiled indulgently on me.

We climbed up a snaking road that lay before us, up and up, to a place where I could see a lake lying below, looking as small as a mill pond. Then the road curved and we were travelling with a sheer cliff on our right, a dizzy drop on the left.

The car gathered speed. I saw Ben's leg move, his foot stabbing the brake. Nothing happened. I think I stopped breathing, for the drop beside me was appalling.

Ben cursed loudly and swiftly changed gear, tearing at the wheel to swing round a bend. The car raced faster, the engine grinding in protest.

'Hold on!' Ben said sharply. 'Hold on tight! Make sure your belt's fastened.'

Ahead, the road levelled for a few hundred yards before plunging steeply. There was a sandy verge at the base of the cliff and Ben swung the car across to it, running along it. The cliff tore at the car, striking sparks, screaming horribly.

And then we saw the outcrop ahead of us. Two feet wide, as tall as the cliff, its edge ragged.

'Oh God!' Ben breathed. 'Oh, dear God!'

I closed my eyes. There was a loud bang and I was thrown forward violently, the belt cutting into me. The world swung round. I heard the ratchet of the hand brake. And then everything stopped. Noise and motion ceased.

I opened my eyes. The car was slewed sideways across the road, its bonnet crunched into the rocky outcrop.

'Get out,' Ben instructed. 'Quickly, Carole. This brake may not hold. If she rolls backwards . . .'

I didn't need telling twice. I was out of the car in a flash and standing in the road trembling. Ben hurried round to me, asking if I were all right and kissing me savagely. Then he wrenched at the crumpled car bonnet and looked at the engine, while I sat down on the dusty verge, careless of my best dress.

A few minutes went by and then I realized that Ben was leaning on the car, staring in disbelief at something in the engine.

'What is it?' I asked. 'Have you found what was wrong?'

'I have,' he said grimly, his face pale and

drawn. 'You were right, Carole. Someone is after my blood. There's a damn great hole in the brake hose. The fluid's been seeping out. The brakes were bound to fail. And it couldn't possibly have been an accident.'

We waited, shaken and not speaking, our hands linked for mutual comfort, until we heard a car coming. Then Ben stepped out to wave the vehicle down before it piled into the Rover.

There were two young couples in the car and they were anxious to help. By bumping and lifting the Rover, we somehow got it up against the cliff with only its nearside wheels on the road. And then Ben asked the other driver to take me to a phone.

'Aren't you coming?' I gasped. 'Ben . . .'

'No, darling. I can't just leave it like this. Phone a garage and have them bring a breakdown truck. Then get a taxi and go home. And ring our friend Mr Jones and tell him what's happened.'

'Mr Jones?' I said stupidly.

Ben frowned. 'Yes, darling, Mr Jones or Mr Lane.'

I understood then. The police. Of course.

Sitting jammed between the two girls, I watched from the back window until Ben was out of sight. I hated to leave him alone. My companions found the whole episode exciting and chatted the whole time until we reached a phone box, and when I had made my calls they insisted on taking me all the way home. They were only out for a ride, they told me gaily, and Trentismere was as good a place as any.

I was left at the top of the drive, feeling unutterably old and weary as the four young people waved back to me. The darkness was closing in. The drive seemed long and lonely, its shadows menacing. I woundered whether Ben was safely at the garage by now.

And then, as I walked slowly down the gloomy driveway, someone hissed at me from among the trees. I came to a standstill, terrified, seeing a figure moving in the shadows.

'Miss Davies!' came an urgent whisper.

Light reflecting dully from his glasses identified Larry Gordan.

'Where's Ben?' he asked. 'Isn't he with you?'

'No, we . . . there was some trouble with the car. What are you doing here?'

'Ssssssh!' he hissed, glancing nervously around him. 'I must see Ben. Come over here.'

I stepped backwards, looking towards the house and wondering if I could reach it before he caught me. Everything seemed clear now. Larry was behind all the trouble. He had opportunity for starting the fire, for planting the bomb, for stealing the plans. He had been around, ostensibly visiting me, shortly before David was attacked. And yesterday I had met him at this same place—with Ben's car

151

standing in the open. Larry could easily have tampered with the brake hose.

But my moment of startled revelation was too long. Larry's boney hand clamped over my wrist. I started to shout, but his other hand came over my mouth.

'Don't scream,' he whispered. 'Please don't. I'm not going to hurt you. I've got to talk to Ben. I've got some information for him. Now I'm going to let you go. If you care at all for Ben, don't make a noise.'

He released me slowly. I didn't scream.

'What's this information?' I demanded in a low voice.

'I can't tell you. Only Ben. Ben'll know what to do. When will he be back?'

'I don't know. The car had to go to a garage. He might be ages.'

Larry groaned softly. 'I can't wait long. I daren't.' He bent over suddenly and picked up a cardboard box fastened with string, thrusting it at me. 'Give him this. He'll understand. And tell him I'll wait in the yard until ten. I've got to see him. Got to.'

'But, Lar . . .' I began. He was gone, slipping away between the trees like a wraith in the dusk.

I stared down at the box in my hands. Whatever it was, I didn't intend giving it to Ben. Nor would I tell him to meet Larry, not now that I knew the truth. It was a trap. And the box . . . it might even be another bomb.

Larry had gone towards the boat-yard. I went the other way, moving swiftly in the uncertain light until I was deep in the woods. Then I flung the box away from me and heard it splash into the lake. It could not harm Ben now, whatever it was.

*   *   *

Astonished stares met me when I walked into the sitting-room. Tom, Sarah and Richard all sat around the table, with a half-made jigsaw puzzle scattered beneath their hands.

The old man looked at my dusty dress and dishevelled appearance and snapped, 'Something's happened. Where's Ben?'

'He's all right,' I said quickly, sinking into a chair. 'Something went wrong with the brake hose, he said. I got a lift and phoned a garage. He shouldn't be too long.'

Tom swung his chair round and brought it across to me, staring into my face. 'An accident?'

'Ben didn't think so. It happened when we were on the pass. If he hadn't thought fast, we would have gone over the edge. The brakes didn't work. Ben scraped the car along the cliff face and we eventually stopped. But the car's an awful mess. He wouldn't leave it. I wanted him to come with me, but . . .'

Tom patted my head self-consciously. 'There now, it's all right. Just relax for a few minutes.'

I lay back and closed my eyes, grateful for the respite. I wanted to tell them my suspicions of Larry, but it would only worry them more. Ben was the one I should share my thoughts with, if only he would listen to me this time.

Any minute, I half expected to hear an explosion from the lake. It would probably go off at ten o'clock, I thought confusedly, since that was the deadline Larry had set himself. No wonder he daren't wait long. By giving me that box he had come into the open. It was lucky for me that he hadn't realized I had guessed his true identity—agent for the people who were determined to stop Ben at all costs.

Looking back on the evening, I know that my thinking was muddled. If my mind had been clear, things might have happened differently, but I was still shaken by our narrow escape from death. That is the only excuse I can offer.

Richard left us shortly before ten, to return to his friends' house in Trentismere village. And soon after he had gone, the telephone rang. Being the most mobile, I reached it first.

'Hello, darling,' came Ben's voice. 'I just phoned to let you know I'm on my way. Sergeant Jones is giving me a lift, so I should be there in about half an hour. O.K.?'

'Fine,' I said relievedly. 'Take care of yourself.'

'And you. 'Bye for now.'

'Was that Ben?' Tom asked from behind me.

'It was,' I said. 'He'll be home soon.'

David was the next to come in, however. He walked into the sitting-room looking pleased with himself.

'You're home early,' he commented to me. 'Did you have another row?'

'They were nearly killed,' Tom growled. 'Somebody's been messing about with the car and they nearly went off the road.'

'What? My God, what next? Are you all right, Carole?'

He wanted to know where Ben was, if he was injured, and then he said it was shocking that such things should go on and the police not do anything about it.

'They're doing their best,' Tom said. 'But after this I think we ought to ask for police protection until they catch the villains. It's getting so a man doesn't feel safe in his own bed.'

'And speaking of bed,' Sarah put in, 'isn't it time you were going? Come on, Carole and I will help you and then when Ben comes you can hold court in comfort.'

He grumbled, but not too fiercely, and we had him installed in his room, propped up by pillows, when Ben arrived.

We stood around Tom's bed for an hour, talking the problem back and forth and getting nowhere. At last I could stand it no longer.

'I think it's Larry,' I burst out.

'Carole,' Ben said wearily. 'I've told you before . . .'

'I know you have, but I'm certain now.' And I enumerated all the incidents and what I saw as Larry's part in them. The four Elliotts listened in silence, Sarah looking worried, Tom wearing a frown, David with a curious glint in his eye, and Ben merely waiting for me to finish, patently not believing a word.

'It's all circumstantial,' he said at length. 'Just because he happened to be around when . . .'

'Then how do you explain what happened tonight?' I demanded.

'It needn't have been Larry who damaged the car. He . . .'

'Not the car. Afterwards. When I came home, he was waiting by the drive—waiting for you. He told me to ask you to meet him in the boat-yard. As if I'd be stupid enough to do that.'

Ben caught me by the shoulders, his eyes blazing. 'Why didn't you tell me this before?'

'Because it was a trap. Anyway, he said he would only wait until ten o'clock and it was long after that when you came home. He'll have gone by now. He must know he's revealed himself.'

Tom was shaking his grizzled head. 'I can't believe it. Not Larry. Why, he thinks the world of Ben.'

'It sounds plausible to me,' Sarah said,

156

shivering.

Ben sighed heavily. 'I'll find out in the morning, when I see Larry.'

The discussion broke up, and Sarah and I went to bed. She needed a little assistance, as her arm was still stiff and sore, but she was soon settled into bed. As I was leaving her room, I heard Ben and David coming up the stairs, arguing as always.

'It's got to be somebody who can hang around without causing suspicion,' David was saying. 'Whoever it is can't just appear out of thin air when he wants to cause mischief. It's got to be Larry.'

'It can't be,' Ben said. 'I just will not believe it of him.'

'Why does he want to see you so desperately, then?'

They paused at the top of the stairs and Ben turned tired eyes on me, asking, 'Did he say why?'

'He said he had information,' I replied. 'He wouldn't tell me what it was, though. He said he could only tell you.'

'You see,' Ben said to his brother. 'Information. He's found out something. And why the devil should he wait for me if he'd tampered with the car. He'd expect me to be dead. So why hang around? And why involve Carole? It would have been simple for him to get me alone some time without specially asking for me. You're both up the creek. It

157

wasn't Larry. We might just as well suspect Arthur Hemmings. Or Richard, or me. Or even Dad, or yourself, or Carole. Or perhaps Sarah's been doing it all by remote control . . . Be your age! Go to bed, for Heaven's sake. I'm sick of talking about it.'

He went into his room and David and I walked on along the landing, wishing each other a subdued goodnight.

The communicating door between Ben's room and mine had been left unlocked since the night when he had failed to come home. Now it stood open and Ben was standing in the doorway.

'I didn't say goodnight to you,' he said, holding out his arms.

When I went to him, he kissed me softly and tenderly, then held me close with his cheek against my hair.

'I'm sorry if I was irritable,' he said, 'but I think this thing is getting on everyone's nerves. I suppose it is possible that you're right about Larry. I'll be on my guard, just in case. And you stop worrying about it. I'm quite able to take care of myself.'

'I hope he doesn't come back,' I said, my face pressed against his shirt front. 'I hope he realises that he can't succeed now. I couldn't bear it if anything happened to you.'

'Nothing will happen to me,' he said confidently, and lifted my mouth to his, so that there was no more room for thought or worry

158

or anything save the glory of being together.

I had completely forgotten about the box.

CHAPTER TWELVE

The following morning, unable to let Ben out of my sight for long, I went out to the boat-yard where he was working and found him standing by a trailer lorry with Arthur Hemmings and Richard Sharp. As I walked across the gravel, Ben came towards me with a harassed look on his face.

'I was just coming to find you,' he said. 'Larry hasn't turned up, so I shall . . .'

'Doesn't that prove that I was right?' I broke in. 'He's run away because . . .'

'I don't know what it proves,' Ben said irritably. 'But it's a damn nuisance. I shall have to go to Bowness with Richard. We've promised to deliver a boat today. And I had enough to do without that.'

'Have you tried to contact Larry?' I asked.

'No. I haven't the time to run after him. But I shall have something to say when he does turn up.'

I stared up at his frowning face and laid a hand on his arm, saying incredulously, 'Ben! You still don't believe that Larry's your enemy, do you?'

'I can't,' he said. 'It doesn't make any sense

159

at all.'

'Then why hasn't he come this morning?' I demanded.

Ben sighed, shaking his curly head. 'I've no idea. And I have other things on my plate at the moment. Let the police handle it.'

'That's what you keep saying. Perhaps I should tell them my suspicions.'

'They'd laugh at you, darling. You can't give them any concrete proof. And they can't use supposition. Let it go for now. If Larry doesn't turn up before I get back, I'll look for him. And if he's left his digs, then we'll see. But don't you fret about it. Will you tell Dad and Sarah not to expect me before late afternoon?'

'I will. But, Ben, please be careful.'

An affectionate smile spread over his face and he bent to kiss me lingeringly, his hands firm on my arms. 'What do you imagine could happen to me?' he asked teasingly. 'Richard will be with me the whole time.'

'Just as I was with you yesterday,' I said bitterly. 'It didn't make any difference then. Perhaps Larry knew that, if he didn't come today, you would have to go on this trip. He might have . . .'

Ben stepped away, flinging out his arms. 'So what do you want me to do? Hide? Or ask for police protection?'

'That isn't a bad idea,' I said.

'Oh, Carole!' Ben sighed. 'I love you for worrying about me, but it isn't necessary. You run along and keep busy and I'll be back before you know it.'

I stood watching until the big power-boat was loaded on to the trailer lorry and the vehicle moved away through the main gates of the yard. I wasn't happy about Ben's trip to Bowness, but there was nothing I could do now. If only he would believe what danger he was in . . .

* * *

I was hoovering the hall when Moira arrived. She stood on the front step, her mouth curving in a smile that blinked out when she saw me.

'Is David in?' she asked, in the curious, nose-turned-up manner I had noted before.

'He's out on the lawn,' I said, coldly polite. 'Would you care to come through?'

She stepped inside the hall and I expected her to walk by, but she paused and gave me a withering look from china-blue eyes.

'I hear you've taken up with Ben,' she said. 'I think you're mad, of course, but I wish you joy.'

'I'm so glad you approve,' I said sarcastically. 'Actually, I think I've got the best of the bargain.'

A tight little smile crossed her mouth. 'Naturally you would think so. But compared to David, Ben is . . .'

'Decent. Kind. And loyal,' I interrupted. 'It

depends on what you admire in a man, of course. I'm sure that David is fine if you're looking for sexual prowess.'

Her red curls danced as she tossed her head. 'I wouldn't know about that. He has never . . .'

'Don't bother lying,' I said. 'I know what David's like, and I'm afraid I saw you when I was out walking the other day. Only a brief glimpse, but it was enough. And you aren't the first by any means.'

'You ought to know,' she said bitterly. 'It may interest you that he's going to marry me as soon as I've worked my notice at the hospital.'

'It doesn't interest me at all, Moira. I only hope he buys you a different engagement ring. The diamond's slightly shop-soiled.'

Hatred darted from her eyes, but she turned a fiery red before she swept away. I wished, too late, that I had refrained from making that last comment. It had been unnecessary, and she probably felt insecure enough without my adding to her pain.

The incident was driven from my mind by a thought which dropped from nowhere. The box Larry had given me, which I had thrown in the lake . . . What was in it? Ben had said that we needed proof of Larry's duplicity. If I could find the box, maybe I would have that proof.

Hurriedly finishing the sweeping of the hall, I waited until David and Moira had driven away in her car, to spend the day together, before making for the lakeside path. I walked

162

along the path twice, scanning the water, but could see no sign of the box.

Certain that I was in reach of a clue, I slipped off my sandals and waded into the cool lake. It was a bright, warm day, but I came out in a cold sweat as I searched the shallows. Something menacing seemed to be in the air. I kept glancing over my shoulder at the peaceful lake and up into the trees growing densely on the hill above me. But only a small breeze was moving.

I thought about the box again. What did it contain? It couldn't have been a bomb or it would have exploded by now. Besides, it wasn't heavy enough. If I had stopped to think about it, I would have realized that at the time. But in my panic I had thought of nothing but ridding myself of the apparent threat to Ben. So what was it?

Then I saw the box, under a ledge of the bank, half submerged. I approached it carefully and lifted it from the water, placing it on the grassy bank and gingerly working at the knots of the string which held on the lid.

At last the string was off. My heart was beating painfully in my throat, my breath came swiftly. I paused to wipe a cold hand across my damp brow. This was it.

I lifted the lid, very slowly, half expecting something to go bang or leap out at me. But nothing happened. A soft bubble of laughter rose up in me and I was glad no one could see me being so afraid of a soggy cardboard box containing layer upon layer of wet squares of newspaper. Could anything be more innocuous?

So great was my relief that it was a few moments before I realized that I would now have to re-think my theory. There was no danger in this box. Had Larry told the truth, after all? Was I entirely wrong?

I tried to remember what he had said about the box—only that I was to give it to Ben, who would understand. Understand what? What could old newspapers tell anyone?

Frowning to myself, I tipped the cuttings out on to the ground. The pile fell in two sections, and in the middle was a small brown envelope with a bulge in it. What was this? A note?

I ripped the envelope open and took out a small object wrapped in tissue paper. And when I unwrapped the paper I sat on the bank, more puzzled than ever, staring down at my open palm, where lay the solitaire diamond engagement ring which I had given back to David.

After sitting there for some time, my brain working feverishly, I jumped to my feet and went in search of my sandals.

*   *   *

When I reached the house, lunch was ready, so I was obliged to delay my investigations until

164

the meal was finished. Of one thing I was sure—I had to talk to Larry. He was the only one who could explain the mystery. I had to find him and make him tell me what his 'information' was.

From Sarah, on the pretext of having a message from Ben, I learned the address of Larry's digs. He rented a room in the village, in a cottage owned by a Mrs Morgan. I was in too much of a hurry to walk, so I commandeered David's car.

As I slowed the Mistrale outside the pretty cottage, I saw a tall, angular woman hoeing the flower beds.

'Mrs Morgan?' I inquired over the hedge.

She came upright, one hand to her back. 'Yes, I'm Mrs Morgan. Can I help you?'

'Is Mr Gordan in?' I asked.

'No, he isn't.' She sounded slightly peeved. 'I haven't seen him since last night. What do you want with him?'

'I had a message for him,' I lied. 'Mr Elliott wondered if he was ill, as he didn't come to work this morning.'

I saw her eyes narrow as she leaned on the hoe, regarding me with puzzlement.

'Mr Elliott's already been here,' she said. 'I told him all I know. Mr Gordan went out about seven last night and hasn't been back since.'

'Mr Elliott was here?' I repeated, astounded. 'When?'

'About eleven, I think. No, wait, it was

165

nearer half past. Apparently Mr Gordan brought a key home from work and Mr Elliott needed it. I let him look through the room and then they went away.'

'They?'

'Mr Elliott and his young lady,' she said patiently. 'Look, miss, if you've come from him you must know all about it.'

'Oh, yes,' I said stupidly, forcing a bright smile. 'But I haven't seen Mr Elliott since early this morning. I must have misunderstood him. You say he searched Mr Gordan's room?'

'For the key, yes. I expect he remembered about it after he'd asked you to call.'

'Yes, that must be it,' I said cheerfully. 'Have you any idea where Mr Gordan will be?'

'None at all. Sorry. But he can't have gone far. All his things are still here. Is there any message I can give him when he comes back?'

'Just ask him to call Miss Davies. And will you please tell him it's urgent? Thank you very much, Mrs Morgan.'

I didn't know whether she believed me, but it didn't matter. I knew what I wanted to know.

It had not, as I had first thought, been Ben who called at the cottage. Especially not with 'his young lady'. Anyway, by eleven, Ben had been on the way to Bowness.

It couldn't have been Tom, either, which left only one 'Mr Elliott'. Had Ben asked David to call at the cottage and find a key? It was unlikely. David was the last person Ben would

166

send on an errand. So what . . .?

Involuntarily, my hand sped to where the ring hung on a locket chain inside my blouse. It wasn't a key David had been looking for, it was the ring. How had David known that Larry had it? Had he given it to the American? Why should he?

I slammed on the Mistrale's brakes and pulled into a lay-by, stricken by the realization of what must have happened to Larry. He must have found out something, something about David, who had given him the ring as a bribe to keep him quiet. But Larry had intended to talk, and I was the one who had told David so. If anything had happened to Larry, it was my fault. David must have . . .

What had David done? What could he do with hands that were raw with burns and enveloped in bandages? He couldn't have set fire to the boat-house, or planted the bomb, or throttled me, or damaged Ben's car. And he certainly hadn't bashed himself over the head.

I relaxed against the seat, relieved that my suspicions could be discounted. As a detective, I was a dismal failure. It wasn't David. He had his bad points, but he wasn't a criminal. Not David.

And then an awful thought struck me. It couldn't be David, unless . . .

I was galvanized into action. Re-starting the engine, I wrenched the Mistrale back on the road, making it scream round the bends as I headed for the house with a desperate plan in mind. One way or another, I would find out the truth.

Going straight to my room, I came out carrying a large handbag and as I hurried back down the stairs Sarah emerged from the kitchen. I had hoped to avoid meeting anyone, but I had a story ready.

'Did you find Larry?' she asked.

'No, he wasn't there,' I said hurriedly. 'I've decided to do some shopping in Carlisle, Sarah. One or two things I need. If David gets back before I do, tell him I hope he doesn't mind my using his car. I'll buy the petrol.'

Sarah blinked at me, looking puzzled. 'All right. But . . .'

'I can't stop,' I said, making for the door. 'Tell Ben I won't be late.'

Taking the road for Penrith, I drove out into the wild moorland and stopped in a lonely valley to change my appearance. David must never know who had been asking questions about him. If I was wrong, it wouldn't matter. But if my new theory was correct, then I had to cover myself.

I put on a wig of short brown hair, tucking my own blonde tresses carefully out of sight. The wig was expensive and made of real hair. It would fool anyone who didn't know me well. Then I plastered make-up on my face—bright blue eyeshadow, scarlet lipstick, black liner round my eyes. And lastly I changed my neat

168

tailored blouse for a low-cut sun-top.

Somewhere on the way to Penrith, I became Elsie Smith.

*   *   *

Elsie liked chewing gum. She found some in the glove compartment and put it in her mouth as she parked the car behind some trees outside the gates of Penrith Hospital. With a jerky, hip-swinging stride that brought whistles from a couple of passing layabouts, Elsie made for the out-patients' department.

The receptionist was a young girl with a mop of fair hair and a bad case of acne. She looked up at Elsie with an unwelcoming stare.

'Yes?'

'Is Moira McRae on duty?' Elsie asked, rolling the gum around her mouth.

The girl's face expressed more interest. 'No, it's her day off.'

'Oh, pity. Do you know her?'

The girl grinned openly. 'Everybody knows Moira. She's something else, isn't she? And now she's gone and got herself engaged to Dave Elliott. You know—the racing driver. He's gorgeous.' She sighed, looking dreamily into the distance.

'Have you seen him, then?' Elsie asked, lounging on the desk.

'Only his photo. In the papers.' The receptionist was leaning forward now, ready to gossip. 'He's smashing! Tall, dark and handsome—the lot. And he must be loaded. Moira's a lucky devil.'

'Weren't you here on Monday when he came in?' Elsie asked.

'When who came in?'

Elsie sighed, the gum smacking in her mouth. 'Dave Elliott. He came to have his dressings changed, didn't he? I could have sworn Moira told me he was in on Monday. He was in an accident, you know. Got his hands burned.'

'Oh, yes, I read about that. But he didn't come in here. At least, I didn't see him. Heck, I hope I didn't miss him. Hang on a minute.' She leapt from her chair and flung open a filing cabinet, swiftly sorting through the files with nimble fingers. Then she turned with a smile. 'I thought not. He wasn't here. There'd have been a card. Anyway, I've been sitting at this desk all week and believe me, if a dream-boat like that had come in, I'd have seen him.'

'Maybe it's next Monday,' Elsie said comfortingly, and turned away.

'Can I give Moira a message?' the girl asked.

'No, don't bother. I'll be seeing her. Thanks.' With a brief smile, Elsie was gone through the door and making her undulating way to the gate.

*　　　*　　　*

The gum was making my jaws ache. I spat it into the gutter and again climbed into the Mistrale, which was getting some curious stares from passers-by. They might remember the unusual car, but the girl to whom I had spoken had not seen me in it, so if David did discover that someone had been asking questions he would not know who it was. Not immediately. Not before I had a chance to do something about it.

I wondered briefly if perhaps he had had his dressings changed at some other hospital, but that was unlikely. Moira had arranged it for him, or so he had said. She would naturally have used the hospital where she worked. But she hadn't. It was all lies. David hadn't had his dressings changed, because he hadn't needed to. He was not as badly burned as he had made us believe. Perhaps he wasn't burned at all. And that answered a lot of questions.

I must go to the police and tell them.

Outside Penrith, I changed back to my own identity and set out for Trentismere. I wondered again what Larry had found out. He must have caught David red-handed, or David would never have given him the ring. Red-handed? My mind caught at the words. Bare-handed, more likely. Had Larry seen David without his bandages? Was that what . . . .?

My foot slammed on the brake and the car stopped with a jerk. I had remembered. I, too, had seen David minus his bandages. If I hadn't been such a fool, I might have known the truth days ago. But I had been so sickened by the sight of David and Moira lying together that I had failed to note the significance of what I had seen, and then it had been driven from my mind because Ben had come home.

What was worse—I had told Moira that I had seen them. She may not have understood what that meant, but David certainly would. When Moira told him . . .

I would be next on his list.

CHAPTER THIRTEEN

I daren't go back to the lake. David was getting desperate. If he had killed Larry, as I was sure he had, then he wouldn't hesitate to murder again.

He was being careless, too. The trip to Mrs Morgan's cottage was his first real mistake, for he must have known that his search of Larry's room would be discovered. When questions were asked about Larry, Mrs Morgan would talk, as she had to me. Ben was sure to find out that David had been there. He would know there was no key. He would know . . .

'Ben?' I whispered to the moors, my hands to my face.

Ben had gone to Bowness. David, too, had gone out, knowing that when Ben came back he would start inquiries about Larry. So David couldn't let Ben reach the cottage. He had to do something quickly. Today. This very afternoon. Perhaps already . . .

I heard myself say, 'No! No! Oh, dear God, please . . .'

*　　*　　*

I was alone, in the middle of nowhere, miles away from Trentismere and any hope of helping Ben. I didn't even know where he would be, unless by some miracle he was at home. Late afternoon, he had said. It was almost five now. Perhaps he was there. Perhaps David hadn't found him yet. It was my only hope. I must get Ben to come to me. When I was sure that he was safe, then we could both go for the police.

I drove on, my eyes blinded to the loveliness of my surroundings, until I came to a phone box standing on a wind-swept shoulder of the hill. There was nothing else in sight but the hills and their stone-wall shawl, a few sheep and the black ribbon of road. Not a house or a sign of human life anywhere.

The phone box was filthy. The directories were missing and the wall and window-panes were covered in obscene graffiti. But the phone worked.

Silently praying to a God I had neglected, I dialled and waited.

'Trentismere two five,' said Ben's voice, distorted by a horrible crackling, but recognizable.

'Oh, darling!' I gasped, my knees feeling weak. 'Are you all right?'

'Of course I am. Where are you?'

'In a phone box. Ben, listen, this is important. I've been making inquiries and I know who it is who's been . . . well, you know . . . doing all those things. I want you to come out here as soon as you can and I'll tell you all about it. Just get out of the house. It's dangerous for you if you stay there. Is David back yet?'

'No.'

'Thank heaven. Can you get a taxi? Please, don't argue, Ben. It's imperative that you come to me.'

'All right, darling,' he said soothingly. 'Where shall I meet you?'

'I'll wait here. I'm about five miles out of Penrith. There's a phone box all by itself, and,' I screwed round, looking out of the window, 'there's a ruin. On the top of the hill. Do you know it?'

'Yes. I'll be there in half an hour.'

'You'll see the Mistrale, anyway,' I said.

'O.K., darling. See you soon.'

I left the box and stood against the door, feeling the headiness of relief run through all my veins. Thank heaven he was safe. And thank heaven he hadn't argued. I must have

174

transmitted my urgency to him. Soon he would be with me.

Meanwhile, though, I had half an hour to while away. I was too edgy to stay still. Leaving the Mistrale by the stone wall, I crossed the road and found a rough track which led up to the ruins.

The path was steep and strewn with dusty stones worn smooth by time and elements and countless feet. It levelled out at the top, on to a roughly circular plateau in the centre of which stood the grey ruins.

A small green notice outside an opening in the broken wall declared, 'National Trust. Ullsdale Castle'. Castle it may have been once, but now it was nothing but an asymmetrical pattern of stone walls, only one of which was tall enough to have a window. After wandering around for a while, with my mind on other things, I sat down on a large stone and lit a cigarette.

Several cars passed on the road beneath me. I could no longer see the Mistrale or the phone box, but for several miles in either direction the road lay to view, winding across the bleak landscape.

In the valley the other side of the road I could see a stream, its bed littered with pale rocks and stones. Beyond it, the further hill rose sharply, muted green and brown, with a wide scree of loose stones falling almost to the valley floor. The sky was a clear hazy blue in

175

the sunlight of late afternoon and there was enough breeze to lift my hair across my face in wisps. I could have enjoyed the tranquillity, if only I could have forgotten the menacing figure of David that seemed to throw a shadow over everything.

At last I saw a black car coming from the direction of Trentismere, coming at what seemed like a slow crawl. I stood up to watch it approach and thought I could detect a 'Taxi' sign in the front window. Then it passed from my sight beneath the hill and I heard it slow down and stop.

I ran to meet him, stumbling in my haste, dropping down the steep track in inelegant leaps. I caught my sandal under a sharp edge and would have gone headlong if I hadn't clutched at a boulder, bruising my knees as I fell. Flushed and panting, my pulse racing erratically, I looked up as a step sounded beneath me. In the same moment, the taxi drew away.

He stood there smiling at me, smiling with his mouth but not his eyes. He was still wearing his bandages.

David.

'Where's Ben?' I said breathlessly, still clutching the rock. 'Where's Ben?'

David's smile died, his features clouded. 'I have bad news for you, Carole. My brother met with an accident this afternoon. It was most unfortunate.'

'You're lying,' I breathed. 'I spoke to him not half an hour ago.'

He shook his head, almost sadly. 'No, Carole. That was me you spoke to. People often confuse his voice and mine over the phone. So you see, whatever you've found out, it's too late. Ben is dead.'

'I don't believe you,' I said desperately.

'No? Then let me tell you the whole thing. I saw it happen. The lorry went off the road and landed upside down, smashed. When the ambulance came, they got Ben out, but it was too late. He was covered in blood. They put him on a stretcher and pulled the sheet up over his face. And one of them said, "We couldn't have done anything for him, anyway. It's merciful".'

I felt sick. I could picture the scene as if I were there, so clearly that it blotted out the sight of David and the landscape.

He was talking again, but his first words were lost in the mist that threatened to overwhelm me. I heard him say something about Larry and the ring and 'Be sensible, Carole. I don't want to have to hurt you.'

'You . . .' I got out, seeing him clearly again. 'You murderer!'

His face tightened with anger. 'I'm asking you to be sensible. It's too late for you to save Ben. Keep your mouth shut and you'll be all right.'

I wouldn't, though. He didn't dare leave me

177

alive with all I knew. If I could just get to the Mistrale . . .

Leaping to my feet, I ran, along the hillside. David shouted and came after me. I glanced over my shoulder. My foot slipped. I slithered and rolled, landing with a thud at the side of the road. I saw David loom above me, outlined against the pale sky. He came down the hill like a mountain goat. Then I was up and running. To the car. Round to the driver's side. Wrenching the door open.

The ignition keys were gone.

Still holding the door, I glanced back along the road. David was walking towards me, unhurriedly, pulling off his bandages as though they had been gloves. He held up one hand, dangling the car keys in the air.

'I thought you might try that. Sorry, Carole. You can't escape. You might as well tell me where Larry put the ring. I know he told you about it. It was stupid of you to mention it to Moira.'

'I didn't . . .' Suddenly, I wanted to laugh. Moira hadn't told him I had seen them making love, she had told him what I said about the ring. An innocent, though catty, remark had led David to guess near the truth. But when I spoke to Moira I hadn't even found the ring. It was very funny. Very funny.

'Where is it?' David demanded, facing me across the gleaming car roof.

'I gave it to the police,' I said.

'You're lying! If you'd done that, they would have been waiting for me. Don't play games with me.' His hand came up and rested on the car. In it was a small and deadly gun.

'If you kill me, you'll never find it,' I said evenly, acutely conscious of the diamond hanging heavy on my breast.

'I can always say Larry stole it,' David replied. 'I don't want to kill you, Carole. Play it my way and . . .'

'And what? Will you bribe me like you did Larry? Oh, no, David. Go ahead and kill me. How will you explain that away?'

David shrugged. 'I won't need to. I told Dad and Sarah that the phone call was from Moira. They think I'm with her. It will be assumed that you died by the same mysterious hand that caused the other troubles—Ben's rivals. They got desperate.'

'The taxi-driver knows you came here,' I said. 'And how will you get back? Everyone knows I'm using the Mistrale, so you can't turn up in it. You aren't supposed to be able to drive.'

'I shall say you called because you thought you were in danger, but you didn't want the others to worry so you asked me to say it was Moira who phoned. I valiantly came out here to aid you and found your poor shattered body. And I don't have to go anywhere. You've kindly provided a phone box which I can use. You see, Carole, I couldn't possibly be a suspect. My hands are useless, aren't they?'

He seemed to have every avenue covered. I had to keep him talking until I thought of something. Perhaps a car would come along.

'Why did you bring me into this?' I demanded. 'You could have come to Trentismere on your own.'

'You were stage dressing. I wanted to plead my forthcoming marriage when I asked for money. That was all I intended to do. But you welshed on me. I soon saw how things were going, so I thought I'd get rid of the boat. It was using up money that I needed. But even that didn't help. I had to get rid of Ben. You heard what the old man said—without Ben, he'd have to sell up. Turn his assets into cash, which I need. It was the only thing I could do. And I did try and make you leave so you wouldn't get mixed up in this, didn't I?'

I stared at him unseeingly, the shock of what he had told me beginning to reach my conscious mind. Without Ben. An accident. Ben is dead. Covered in blood. The sheet over his face. Ben is dead. Ben is dead. My last control snapped.

I turned and scrambled over the low wall, running down the hill. Running I knew not where. Only to get away. But not from David. To get away from the voice inside me that cried unbearably for Ben.

Each step jolted my entire being. My legs were like lead, my eyes aching with unshed tears.

At the bottom of the hill I splashed through the stream and began to climb the far side up to the scree. The stones slipped from beneath me as I scrambled up, and I heard them rolling and bumping down behind me. Twice I slid backwards only to claw my way up again, trying to reach the top and run, run, for ever.

And then I heard a car coming along the road.

I turned round, sitting down with a bump. But the car was too far away. If the occupants noticed us at all, they would probably take us for a courting couple out for a ramble. The vehicle didn't even pause in its journey.

I became aware that David was beneath me on the hill, using one hand for climbing while the other held the gun still pointed at me. I took a handful of the loose stones and flung them at his upturned face.

His handsome features distorted with rage. He steadied the gun and squeezed. The bullet swept past my shoulder.

Suddenly I hated him with murderous intensity. Let him kill me. If Ben was dead, I didn't care about living. But first I would hurt him, mark him, so that someone would know the truth.

We were well up the hill. The drop was very steep and dangerous with all the sliding stones and dust of the scree. I let David get closer. One step. Two. Then I stood up and leapt, feet first, right into him.

We went together, tangled arms and legs lurching through the air, bumping and sliding. I was helpless. The stones cut me all over as we tumbled headlong. I heard David yelp and curse. Then, with a final thump, we stopped. The air deserted my lungs and for a moment I lay dazed and gasping for breath.

Orange candy-floss clouds lazed in the washed-blue sky. I felt the sun and the breeze on my face as the earth resumed its rightful place beneath me. And there was a heavy weight lying across my middle, pressing me into the sharp stones.

I pushed myself up painfully with my elbows and stared without understanding at the still form of David. He lay on his face, humped over me, one arm flung above his head, the other doubled beneath him. Something wet and warm was spreading over my skirt. As I felt it seep through to my flesh I shuddered and frantically pushed David away from me, pulling my legs out from beneath the weight of him. My clothes were covered in blood.

David rolled over, gently. His right hand, still loosely holding the gun, flopped out and splashed into the stream, reddening it with his blood. I had not heard the gun go off, but it had done. The bullet had caught David in the stomach and gone right through him, tearing a great gaping hole in his side.

I saw all these details in one horrified

glance. Then I turned away and was sick, sick as I had never been before, sick until the retching threatened to tear me inside out, until my eyes were blinded with tears, until my head was thumping and every muscle aching intolerably.

When it was over, I crawled to the stream and plunged my face into the icy water. I rubbed the cold wetness into my arms and legs, making them sting at every cut and scratch. But nothing seemed real. What was I to do now? Where was I to go?

I glanced back at David. He lay as before, his eyes staring sightlessly at the arch of sky, his face ashen.

Ben, I thought, and I stood up. I needed Ben. He was the only one who . . . And then I remembered. I could never again run to Ben, to the comfort of his arms, the warmth of him.

Ben was dead.

I stood there swaying, trying to think clearly. But all I could think of was the picture of Ben lying mutilated in the wreckage of the trailer lorry. The pain inside me was unbearable.

How long I stood there I don't know, but eventually a semblance of sanity came back to me and I knew that I must move. I must get to the phone box and let someone know what had happened. It didn't really seem to matter any more, but I made myself start walking.

I was staggering like a drunkard, but if I stopped I knew the trembling would make me want to lie down and never get up. Lifting tear-misted eyes to the vague red oblong I could just see at the top of the slope, I went on, forcing one foot in front of the other. It seemed a long, long way, and somehow I wished I could never get there, that I could go on like this, not thinking, not feeling.

The hill seemed to tilt in front of me until it was almost perpendicular. I felt my senses slipping from me. I was so weary, so very weary. I wasn't going to make it.

A sound penetrated my fuddled brain. The sound of a car engine. I heard a sharp slam. Through the thickening mist in my mind I saw a figure appear beyond the wall.

I heard a voice, way off, calling my name.

And then I knew what it was. I was dying. And Ben had come to meet me.

Knowing utter peace and contentment, I gave myself to the white mist.

CHAPTER FOURTEEN

I remember coming slowly back to consciousness. My first memory is of birds singing and leaves rustling. I was warm and comfortable, at peace.

Then something clattered nearby. I forced my eyes open, seeing nothing but a bright haze at first, then noting a bottle hanging above my head—a bottle full of colourless liquid that was dripping down a tube. My gaze followed the tube down to where it entered my arm. I was in hospital.

Venetian blinds across the open window let in strips of sunlight that fell across the back of a dark-haired girl in nurse's uniform, who was doing something on a trolley. I was reminded of Moira, and from that came memories of everything that had happened. I was alive. But I didn't want to be alive. Not without Ben.

Warm tears dripped down my temples into my hair and a muffled sob broke from my lips. I saw the nurse turn, then she darted to the wall and pressed a button before coming to bend over me.

'Miss Davies? How are you feeling? Come on, now. Don't cry. You're going to be fine.'

She wiped my eyes with a tissue and smiled at me. 'It's all over. You had a nasty shock, but . . .' She turned as the door opened and a man came in. He had a bald head and a paunch and he looked severely at me.

'About time, too. You haven't been co-operating at all, young lady.' Firm fingers felt for my pulse. He listened to my heart and looked in my eyes.

'Not a thing wrong with you. You just couldn't be bothered to fight, could you? But you will now. You're young and strong. The world is waiting.'

I closed my eyes, willing him to go away. I

couldn't face the thought of the world, waiting, with questions, flash bulbs, and microphones. And no Ben.

The doctor said quietly, 'Why don't you want to live, Miss Davies? You can, you know. There's nothing physically wrong with you. Yet you've been lying here for a week without a sign of . . .'

My eyelids flew open. A week? Seven days? Was he crazy?

He nodded sagely. 'A week. Had us all wracking our brains for the reason, and running around like scalded rabbits to try and bring you back to us. Don't we deserve a little help from you? Would you like to sit up?'

No, said my brain. Move or speak and you've had it. You won't be able to slip back into the mist. The mist was where Ben was, waiting for me.

But the mist was receding rapidly and the none-too-gentle hands that pulled me up and made me stay there until the pillow was raised dispelled it entirely.

'That's more like it,' the doctor said. 'Go ahead and glare at me. I want you to get involved again. Any kind of feeling is good for you. Don't you care about the people who are worrying over you? Mr Elliott. And your mother.'

'My mother?' I said clearly, startling myself.

'She came as soon as she heard. All the way from Sussex.'

'My mother?' I said again, and began to laugh softly. It was just too funny. I had nearly to die before mother showed interest. Had she left dear Henry to fend for himself for once?

The doctor grinned with me, showing large white teeth. 'Nurse,' he said, 'fetch Miss Davies a cup of tea.' And then he became sober again. 'It isn't funny really. Your mother's been out of her mind with anxiety. She blames herself for your illness.'

I stopped laughing. It was unkind of me. I must be grateful for anything I could salvage out of the awful mess of my life. I was beginning to accept the fact of my continued existence.

'Have they ...' I said, the words nearly choking me. 'Have they had the ... the funeral?'

The bald head nodded lugubriously. 'On Monday. It was a terrible business, and an awful shock for everyone, especially you. But it's over now. You must look to the future.'

It's over. That was what the nurse had said, too. But it wasn't over. It had only just begun—life in a world that didn't contain Ben. Where had they put him? Was he at Trentismere, near the lake? He would want to be near the lake. Poor Tom. Poor Sarah. Poor Carole.

I was weeping again, quietly, the tears just rolling gently down my face.

The doctor put his hand on my arm, saying

187

softly, 'What is it, my dear? Did you care for him?'

'Care?' I cried. 'Care? He was everything to me. Why should I want to live? What is there for me without him?'

The nurse came back at that moment, with the tea. I dried my face and whispered my apologies to the doctor and he patted my arm understandingly before handing me the cup.

'I phoned Mr Elliott,' the nurse said, smiling at me. 'He's coming right away, with your mother.'

Dear Tom, I thought. He was still being kind to me in the midst of his sorrow.

'Is mother staying with them?' I asked.

'I believe so,' said the doctor. 'They would both have camped here if we had let them.' He gave me a puzzled look and added, 'I don't think that young man has slept a wink since you were brought in.'

'Young man?' I repeated stupidly. 'What young man?'

'The one we're talking about—Mr Elliott. Ben, isn't it? I understood that your involvement with his brother was over. I don't think he knows . . .'

'Ben is dead,' I said quietly. 'I know that. Don't try to spare me. David told me all about the accident.'

'Ben is alive,' the doctor stated. 'He's been here every day since . . .

'Then whose funeral did you . . .?' I began,

and stopped with my mouth open. Not Ben. David. David had had to be buried. It was David's funeral.

The wondrous truth began to seep into my incredulous being. Ben wasn't dead.

'He's alive?' I whispered. 'Is he? He's all right?'

'He's half crazy with worry,' the doctor said, 'but apart from that he's fine. What's all this about an accident?'

'David said . . .' David. Oh, the wickedness of him. He was never through with trying to hurt people. He had lied deliberately and by doing so had almost succeeded in killing me.

But I had come back to life despite him. He was denied his last victory. Let him roast in hell, knowing that Ben and I were together. Ben and I. Ben . . .

'How soon will he be here?' I asked, sitting up.

Nurse Anderson helped me change from the cotton hospital gown to a frilly white nightdress which she said Ben had brought along with other things from my room at Trentismere. I didn't tell her that the nightdress was a new one which I had never seen before. She brushed out my hair and gave me a mirror and a lipstick which I applied sparingly, noting woefully that I looked awful. My skin was sickly pale and there were dark bruises under my eyes.

And then she opened the drawer of the

bedside cabinet and took out something which she held in the air, saying, 'Is this your engagement ring? You had it on a chain round your neck.'

The sight of the ring made me shiver. I disowned it and asked her to put it back in the drawer.

I could hardly believe that it was a whole week since I had fought with David on the hill. Few traces remained of my tumble down the scree, only faint vestiges of the deeper cuts. A week. And Ben had spent that week worrying, on top of all the trouble there must have been about David. What an awful week it had been for him.

Then the door came open and Ben was standing there with a look of hope on his dear, tired face. He was thin, so painfully thin I wanted to cry. While I was busy being sorry for myself, he had been through hell.

The nurse smiled at me and slipped out of the room.

'Oh, Ben!' I choked, holding out my arms.

He took two jerky strides and gathered me to him, holding me so tightly that I felt my ribs must break. His mouth came on mine with a hurting fierceness and I found the Heaven I had thought lost.

He was allowed only five minutes and we said very little in that time, only silly things that lovers the world over say to each other, but I don't believe that any two people ever knew the same soaring gladness that we shared in those moments.

'I'm sorry,' said a voice from the door. It was the doctor again. 'Five minutes is all I can allow you today. She needs a lot of rest yet.'

Ben swiftly stood up, his hand squeezing mine as he faced the doctor. 'Of course. Is Mrs Hayes there?'

The doctor pulled the door wider and mother came in, wearing an atrocious red hat and a woe-begone expression.

'Carole, dear. I'm so glad. We've been so worried.'

I held out my free hand to her, with a warm feeling of benevolence towards the whole world. 'Thank you for coming, mother.'

She came and took my proffered hand, bending to kiss my cheek. 'It's all too terrible,' she said, dabbing her eyes with a wisp of lace. 'I can hardly believe that David . . . He seemed so nice.'

'You only met him once,' I reminded her. 'How's Henry?'

She let go of my hand and squared her shoulders, ready to leap to her husband's defence.

'I mean it,' I said. 'Is he well?'

'Yes, but . . . Well, I shall have to go back now that I know you're going to be all right. Henry hates being alone in the house. And you do have Ben.'

'Yes,' I said, smiling up at Ben, who was

watching me as if I were a plate of beef and he a starving man. 'I have Ben. Mother, will you tell Henry I'd like to be friends with him?'

'Well,' she said dubiously, 'I'll tell him, but . . .'

'Don't you want us to be able to bring your grandchildren to see you?' I asked.

Mother glanced across the bed at Ben, looking embarrassed, and said, 'Goodbye, Carole. Take care of yourself.'

The doctor started to say something, but Ben nodded, said, 'I'm coming,' and bent to kiss me hard, but briefly, before making for the door.

*   *   *

It was not until late the following morning, when I woke after a restful sleep, that I realized there were things I still did not know. I could hardly wait for Ben to come. But first I had another visitor—Detective Sergeant Jones.

He made me tell him everything I had done on that last day. When I mentioned the diamond ring, he asked for it. It was needed as evidence, and I was only too glad to be rid of it at last.

He left me before I had a chance to start asking questions.

A clock somewhere outside my window was chiming two when Ben walked through the door, his arms full of flowers, fruit and chocolates and a wide grin on his face.

'You look better,' he said.

'So do you,' I replied. 'Did you have a good sleep?'

'The best ever. And dreams. You'd blush if you knew the dreams I had.'

'As long as they were about me,' I said happily.

He dumped his burdens at the end of the bed and came to kiss me longingly, his hands either side of my face. Then he leaned away and studied my face for a moment.

'I'm so relieved you're all right,' he said. 'When I first saw you on the moors I thought you were dying. You should have seen yourself—blood all over, your clothes torn, covered in dust.'

'Then you were there,' I said wonderingly. 'I thought I saw you, but . . . how did you know where I was?'

'I'd better start at the beginning,' Ben said, settling himself on the bed with my hands caught between his. 'It seems that Larry was out walking and stumbled across Dave and Moira. They were in a compromising position and Dave had shed his bandages. He wasn't burned much at all.'

'I know,' I said. 'Go on.'

'Dave gave Larry the ring—your ring—to keep him quiet. He swore he wouldn't tell what he had seen, but he must have known it would

193

be important to me. He saw you, and then he waited in the yard, where Dave found him and guessed what he was doing. Moira says Dave didn't intend to kill him, but Larry was so scared he dropped dead the minute Dave laid hands on him. The autopsy bore that out. He died of a heart attack.'

'Did you say Moira told you all this?' I asked.

'Not me. The police. But I'm coming to that in a minute . . . They hid Larry's body in the woods, among the bracken. He hadn't got the ring with him, so the following morning they searched his room at the cottage.'

'I thought so,' I said. 'It wasn't there, was it?'

'No. It's never been found.'

'It has now. I had it.'

'You?' Ben raised his eyebrows. 'How come?'

'Later,' I said impatiently. 'You were telling me about you.'

'Oh . . . yes. Well, I was in Bowness, as you know. I didn't get back till about five and then I went straight to Mrs Morgan's to see if Larry was home. He wasn't, naturally, but Mrs Morgan told me about her visitors—a tall man with a red-haired girl and later a blonde girl who acted a bit scatty.'

I made a face at him and Ben laughed. 'That's what she said. She also told me the man had been looking for a key, so I went home to ask Dave what he was playing at. I arrived just

194

after he'd gone out in a taxi, supposedly to meet Moira, but when I went round to Moira's house she was still there.

'I was getting a bit windy by this time. You'd been behaving oddly, from all accounts, and you weren't home yet. And now Dave had gone on some mysterious errand . . . Anyway, I talked to the taxi-driver when he got back to the village and he told me where he'd taken Dave. He also said there was a pale blue sports car parked by the phone box. I knew you were using the Mistrale, so I guessed who Dave was meeting. And while we're on the subject, why did you ask him to meet you?'

'I thought it was you I spoke to,' I said, lifting his hand to my face. 'He pretended to be you. The last person in the world I wanted was David. I even told him I knew something. He came to shut me up.'

Ben's arm came round me, pressing me close to him. 'Thank God he didn't. Thank God.'

'So you did come to find me,' I said. 'I'm so glad. And then what?'

'Then I called the police. And an ambulance. When Moira heard that Dave was dead, she was only too eager to talk. She hadn't really believed he would sink to murder and she was willing to go along with him in anything else. She was in it from the night of the fire. He promised to marry her if she would help him. She even hit him over the head when he told her to. And now she'll have to face a trial alone . . . Poor Moira.'

'Poor Eva Braun,' I said quietly.

Ben put one finger beneath my chin and lifted my face until our eyes met. 'Now it's your turn,' he said. 'I want to know everything. Why did you go to Mrs Morgan? What were you doing on the moor? And how in heaven's name did you get the ring?'

So I began to tell him the story of that last day. Sitting in the safety of Ben's arms, it was hard to credit that what I was saying had really happened. It seemed like a story.

*   *   *

Ben and I were married quietly as soon as I left the hospital. With every day that has passed since that time, David's wickedness becomes more and more unreal. The house by the lake is full of love and laughter and, although I sometimes see Tom staring across the water with a bleak expression, as if he is remembering, I feel sure that soon he, too, will forget his pain. And then the shadow will be gone from Trentismere. For ever.